BEFORE THERE WERE FLOWERS

This book is a work of fiction. The names, characters and events in this book are the products of the author's imagination or are used fictitiously. Any similarity to real persons living or dead is coincidental and not intended by the author.

The content associated with this book is the sole work and responsibility of the author. Gatekeeper Press had no involvement in the generation of this content.

Before There Were Flowers

Published by Gatekeeper Press
7853 Gunn Hwy., Suite 209
Tampa, FL 33626
www.GatekeeperPress.com

Copyright © 2024 by Benjamin Shepherd

All rights reserved. Neither this book, nor any parts within it may be sold or reproduced in any form or by any electronic or mechanical means, including information storage and retrieval systems, without permission in writing from the author. The only exception is by a reviewer, who may quote short excerpts in a review.

Library of Congress Control Number: 2024940751

ISBN (paperback): 9781662952456
eISBN: 9781662952463

BEFORE THERE WERE FLOWERS

Benjamin Shepherd

Tampa, Florida

CONTENTS

Introduction	1
A Ship of Ethereal Wings	3
The Orphan and The Caterpillar	5
The Bogong Moth	6
The Royal Adonis	8
The Eyes of Truth	10
Parle the Cost of Freedom	12
Gastropoda	14
The Terms and Conditions of Freedom	16
The Ceremony of Freedom	19
How Were Flowers Made	21
There is No Future, There is No Past	24
Not All Choose Freedom	27
Potential	29
Balance	31
Control is Not Love	33
A Changed Visage	35
Lions in the Dunes	37
The Greatest of Elements	39
The Spider Queen	42
Ancient Warriors	44
The Wharthog	46
Riposo	49
The Eternal Fountain	51
A Friend of Garbo's	53
The Language of Every Heart	55
Two Hearts Collide	58
Theridiidae	60
The Salt Lord	62
The Foundation of Love	64
Diamond Back	66
The Princess of Cats	69
The Sacred Ornaments	73
Simplicity of Innocence	75

CONTENTS

A Deep Keeled Vessel	77
We Gather Faith	79
Practice Our Movements	81
The Evil Eye	83
Silence	85
Purge Out The Flies	86
The Salt Blade	89
Your Actions Are Misunderstood	93
Diamond Back	95
Moglie	97
My Queen	98
The Queen of The New Moon	100
The Queen Removes Her Armor	103
A Catalyst	106
The A Relationship	108
Self Care	110
A History	112
A Water Better Than Nectar	115
Unto Death	117
What are You Saying	121
The Villa of Awareness	122
The Lion's Den	124
The Voice of Knowledge	126
The Sirens of Sea Glass	127
My Duty	129
A Kingdom is A Birthright	131
A Perfect Lie	132
Free Will	134
Messengers of Light	139
Faith Plus Awareness	142
Commander of Tides	145
The Dream State	147
Epilogue	151
Credits	153

Before There Were Flowers

INTRODUCTION

The god Icarus slept, and while dreaming, wings of feathers and beeswax became part of him. Escaping his prison in Sicily, he flew too close to the sun. The beeswax melted and dripped into my dreams.

A lung disease held me in a prison of sleep for eight weeks beside the sea in Sicily. I dreamed this story and would wake long enough to write it down; then, like Icarus, the beeswax of my wings fell across these pages, and I plunged again into the wine-blue sea of dreams.

Before There Were Flowers

CHAPTER 1
"A SHIP OF ETHEREAL WINGS"

"Sir, we've sighted the ship."

"Well, now, Sir, begging your pardon. I wonder if we have. There you see."

"Look again, Sailors."

"I've lost It, but swear it was there, Sir."

"And you, Moglie?"

"Well, Captain. I'm not a gentleman sailor; I'm just serving Her Majesty's service, protecting the sugar. A humble man I am." The captain took the brass glass from the first mate's hands.

"Your tongue, Moglie, is captured with bars of Ivory and surrounded by a wall of flesh for a reason. Now, where is the ship hiding?"

"Well, Sir, do you see the current change out yonder?" The captain peered to the horizon. "By all my years aboard the Wasp, that is the marriage of the Atlantic and Caribbean Sea. Now, I'm no gentleman sailor, Sir." The captain turned his head and bit his tongue at Moglie. "The squall, Sir." The image of rain low upon the sea appeared in the captain's aperture.

"Common to all waters, Moglie."

"Yes, yes, too true, but you see, Sir. To my pillaged eyes, it morphs into shapes of sails at times."

"It's gone."

"Well, yes, Sir, that's what I'm saying. One moment it's there, and another it ain't, and sometimes a squall, and times it ain't."

"How do they mask themselves? I'm asking Moglie, this is the time to use your tongue."

"Well, they're not entirely humankind, Sir. More mothish."

"They have wings?"

"Oh yes, Sir, and teeth."

"But the ship is real?"

"Hmm, well, hard to say for true, Sir."

"Tomlin! Eyes on that cloud and bring us upon its stern. Prepare the forward guns."

"Captain, it's a mere squall on the horizon." In a flash, the captain brought the tip of a small dagger to the throat of the first mate. "A squall that may kill you. Question me again and lose an ear." The captain turned back to the rail. "Moths?"

"Aye, Captain, and butterflies. You see that way; some sleep the day and some the night. The ship ever traversing, feeding, gathering for the Mother Queen."

"And you know this how?"

"Marked me he did, the King. Aye, nine years ago." A visage of faint lines and colors crossed the sailor's chest.

"He trusted you?"

"Ahh, I wouldn't say that. Prisoner I was, Sir." The captain looked at Moglie for truth and then back at the cloud.

"Fool, I am. Tomlin, fire two salvos into the cloud and prepare to alter course."

"Fire into a cloud, Captain?" Like the thunderbolt of Zeus, so leaped the captain's arm, and blood burst from the ear of the first mate. The shots loosed, and the captain stared into the squall, as if small particles of the cloud broke off. "Again, Tomlin! Is it him, Moglie?

"Aye, it is. Pray it the King and not the Spider Queen."

"Where are you fleeing? Stand up, Sailor."

"You don't catch the Devil, Sir. The Devil catches you, and I'm no vegetable, and the queen eats meat." Moglie unleashed a knife and cut through the glove of the captain's hand.

"Captain, the cloud has vanished, Sir." The captain turned and looked forward as a shadow eclipsed the sun. "Above us, Sir!" The captain slowly raised his head as water engulfed him from the keel of a cloud. Vast blue wings billowed above them.

"The God of Peru, Sir!"

"Aye, a ship of ethereal wings."

Before There Were Flowers

CHAPTER 2
"The Orphan and the Caterpillar"

"Permiso, permiso, shh! Permiso-ish. Nectarish is goodish. I singish to the nectarish. Te amoish." The wooden legs of the ancient man tapped across the cobblestones. Bannered with colors of sea and coral, the arms protruded from a coat of many layers. The fingers protruded from the palm as sticks of fibrous vegetables able to clasp individual sweet fruits and bend them towards the mouth.

"Fish for sale."

The creature cocked his head toward the small voice and staggered toward the orphanage market where many traded. "Pesce? Pescish, fish-ish, wishes?"

"Why the fish weights in your beard, old man? Do they draw your jaws down and make you speak like that?" They wobbled straightened on the pegs and squinted two beaded eyes at the orphan selling fish. The puppet arms held the tubers of vegetables upright as if dancing to a flute. The corded beard dripped with nectar.

"These little dillies are pearls, and my speech is quite impeccable." The fingers fumbled the coarse fibers running through the black pearls. Then Pilgrim's fingers crossed the brim of his slickered hat, and there pasted gold coins to each finger. He waved a kaleidoscope of reflecting color before the orphan selling sardines. "Is the priest still here-ish?" The Orphan peered into the drawn eyes, and the Pilgrim showed his teeth and nibbled, mocking a rat at the juice. "That priest-ish?" The orphan nodded, knowing who the creature meant. "Goodish." The Pilgrim spun the fingers like a shepherd's hook and motioned the boy to follow him.

CHAPTER 3
"THE BOGONG MOTH"

"Atlas, the captain approaches with the last of the cargo. Prepare to retrieve the long boat and weigh anchor."

"Aye, Bogong."

Beings moved about the Ship, silent as soft breezes.

"Polyphemus, prepare to retrieve the longboat."

"Captain Morpho looks weary, no Bogong?"

"Yes, the Ship is nearly full. This is the last orphan the queen requested." His cape of wood colors lifted, and the white eyes on his back distinguished him from the night.

"Divination? Is that how she does it, Bogong?"

"You are young. You will learn much as we reach the Gold Coast. Now, Morpho approaches be ready. The orphan is still young enough for the gold spell to work. He will not be so in a few days. Morpho must rest or die."

"Diamond Back told me he was immortal."

"Diamond Back? The Ship's physician has not been long with us. Captain Morpho's immortality is given by the queen. The closer he is to her, the more protection he has. At this distance, he is deteriorating quickly. He must rest or die. Prepare his bed."

"And nectar for him?" Bogong turned starlight, reflecting in obsidian eyes.

"No, of nectar, he's had quite enough. As I said, he's deteriorated."

"Release the ship, Captain." Morpho peered into the reflecting eyes of Atlas and was mesmerized by his own reflection. "His muscles are beginning to seize."

"Bogong?"

"I am here."

"The Orphan-ish. He must not be with the others."

"I understand. Though, is it necessary to bind him?"

"Yes-ish. He's different. I could feel it. His day is nigh, and he may destroy us all."

"Does he have that strength?" Morpho lurched as if two hearts were beating within him.

"No-ish, He's still a boy, yet. We must seek a greater power with haste-ish. Bogong, he is mightier than thee-ish. Let only Adonis near him and stave a distance, yet-ish." Morpho's peg legs sprouted suckers that seized the ship's deck, and for once, he stood mast like in the night.

"He's seizing! Call for Diamond Back. Atlas, son, quick again with your wing." The captain collapsed.

"Bogong, Bogong," guttural noise emerged.

"I'm here, Captain. My cloak and sword are thine."

"Seek the greater power. Set course for Gastropoda."

CHAPTER 4
"THE ROYAL ADONIS"

"This food is good. It's more fulfilling than what the priest feeds us." Adonis, in royal colors, bowed before the orphan.

"It's what your body needs."

"Is it what your body needs? We are different, right?"

"Are we?" The orphan looked at his body and observed no change.

"Is it your job to feed me?"

Adonis lifted, removing a plate made of shell. "It is my pleasure to serve you and to feed all aboard this vessel."

"Slave? Cook? Butterfly? Man? What are you?"

The being swirled the blue cape around him, forming a pillow to sit on.

"Young Master, I am Adonis. Now, tell me your name."

"I am an orphan of the St. Francis; orphans have no names."

"What do you people call you?"

"Market people call me a bastard of a European planter for the fairness of my skin. They say he gave the Priest money to take me. The Priest gives me nothing but lashings and a number. I am Seven."

"Seven?"

"Yes, that is the number he gave me."

"Ahh, the Seventh Orphan de St. Francis."

"Is this a ship of war, Adonis? I ask because I woke to the cannon fire and then the mighty lifting; I've never felt weightless, this whole vessel weightless, like seabirds. I was tethered to this bed then, but I know not why? Do you fear me?"

"I fear thee not."

"I heard the feet of many slaves coming aboard after the cannon fire, after the weightlessness. Their chains being rendered asunder, the rejoicing."

Adonis listened, and the black perimeter of his cape grew in intensity.

"These are not chains nor ropes. This bed is not a cell. I have not been beaten. I have rested and fed and been asked only my name. You have a language. For I have seen its evidence. A language of symbols tattooed appears not only on the walls and beams of the ship but the inside of the shell bowl, the cording of this fibrous rope on the inside of your cloak, and about your belt of arms. Decipher it? No, I cannot. Speak it? No, I have never heard it. I am free, and yet I am your prisoner. So, Adonis, servant of the ship. With your tattooed ropes, your food, your plate of shell glass, your cloak of ever-changing colors, and your flying ship, I command you to speak. Where dost thou take me?"

Adonis rose, sweeping the cloak, and the fibers of the milkweed rope retracted the orphan who was leaving the constraints of the golden spell.

"Soon, Francis. You will be free."

"Bogong?" The tattoos of the companionway walls moved.

"I'm here, Adonis."

"You heard that?"

"Aye."

"How close are we to the Greater Power?"

"By Atlas's eye, we are seven moons."

"Will the queen not pull us to her?"

"She only pushes. She does not pull."

"But we have a full ship, not only of orphans but the slaves. Morpho is decaying, and the power of the seventh orphan is within, now."

"Garbo knows we are coming. I sent Ulysses ahead. Atlas beholds his blue wings with his eye. All is not lost."

"If Morpho…"

"He will not. Come, let's share a cup of nectar."

CHAPTER 5
"THE EYES OF TRUTH"

"May I, Polyphemus?"

"Yes, of course, Atlas. It's your turn to find courage and dry your wings this night."

"I brought you Nectar, brother. Have you eaten?"

"I haven't the appetite. I feel the danger. Tell me, Atlas. How far can you see into the future with your eyes?" The amber being stepped to the ship's bow and looked across the sea.

"Beyond the horizon of the new day."

"And to the past? How far does your gaze cast behind you?"

"To the end of our memories."

"So, you've seen the Gold Coast?"

"I've seen every beings' story of the Gold Coast, yet never been there."

"Even that of Morpho?"

"Yes, Polyphemus, I have seen him as a child in Spain, a soldier of Portugal, a prisoner of the Queen, and now as the King of Peru."

"Ahh, ahh, your burden is significant."

"We were all once slaves but not all warriors."

"You mean you see the stories of all these?" Polyphemus spread his ethereal wings, and in the moonlight, blue calligraphy filled the inside of the cape.

"Yes, but not only of the warriors but of slaves." Atlas echoed his wings over the ship, and in the moonlight, the deck glowed in gold calligraphy of every slave the vessel had ever saved.

"Ahh, vast wisdom comes from past pain. You bear the mark. Morpho trusts you."

"Brother, we all carry the mark, save one."

"The physician. And what can you see of his past?"

"He is shielded by a skeleton different than ours. Made from knowledge rather than wisdom. He is cunning and only saves those he deems valuable to the ship."

"He discriminates care?"

"In his surgery, he plays God. Of his origins, I can see nothing."

"You cannot see his story?"

"My eyes can only see the truth." Polyphemus took the shoulders of Atlas.

"By my cape and sword, what are you saying? What, is he without a past?"

"I'm saying he changed into something new to hide his past."

"Atlas. Diamond Back morphs?"

CHAPTER 6
"Parle the Cost of Freedom"

"Bogong, I have seen Ulysses, and he has changed the color of his wings."

"Very good. We have been granted safe passage to Gastropoda."

"He does not stand alone. The giant and ancient giant stand with him in the radiant sun."

"Ahh, Garbo and Bianchi! Good fortune at last!"

"First light of the new day, the God of Peru will be in her harbors, Sir."

"These, yes, these are good tidings. I must take them to Morpho."

"Shall I explain the Terms and Conditions of Freedom to our passengers?"

"Mmm, yes. Better to do so in the darkest hour than in the radiant light of hope. Parle the cost of Freedom."

"And the orphan?" Bogong turned his wood-colored cloak.

"No, he is under the care of Adonis. The boy has been steeped in the lies of the priest. Adonis is sorting through his knowledge. Casting away what lies and replacing it with wisdom. He will be ready to disembark on the morrow. Once to Gastropoda, he will be taken in the care of the greater power. The Giant Snails will heal the Child." Atlas turned to go.

"Sir, how is our King, Morpho?"

Morpho lay on his stomach. The plates of his heavy coat ridged his back. The face turned into pillows, and the arms and legs protruded.

"Has he taken much nectar, Adonis?"

"Ha, much nectar. There's not enough nectar in all Gastropoda to slick his thirst. What is he working through?"

Bogong turned his eyes to the blue Adonis.

"The past."

"For all he has drunk, he does not seem weary of it."

"No, it only dulls his pain. It doesn't heal it."

"Diamond Back says it's a condition of his heart, his mind perhaps. Even though his body deteriorates, his inner being is quite intact. I'm seeking understanding, Bogong."

"Diamond Back. He has provided service?"

"Yes! Excellent service."

"Yes, of course."

"What is this burden of the heart he carries?" Bogong pulls out a chair.

"Morpho is a soldier and is duty-bound to the Queen, and yet he is her lover, the father of the child, Luna."

"What? Surely, you jest. Bogong. The Queen emolliates her lovers daily. That's why she's called the spider. I've seen it with my own eyes."

"Yes, tarry a while, and I will tell you the story of their love."

CHAPTER 7
"Gastropoda"

"Adonis, are these whales?"

"Ahh, welcome, Seven of Francis. Be careful now whilst stretching your legs. This is the God of Peru, and we are entering the harbor of Gastropoda. Land of the Giant Snails."

"I've never seen a proper whale before and so many at once."

"Whales, dolphins, turtles. They are our protectors here. They grant us safe passage to this place covering our wake so our enemies cannot follow our sea trail."

"Enemies? Oh yes, the cannon fire but can't they see you?"

Adonis whirled his blue cape wing in front of him and vanished behind a mirror reflecting the world.

"Doubtless, this is how the ship flies. You all have such traits as this?" Adonis stretched his arm toward the blue whale beside the vessel, and it rolled and lifted an enormous eye and took in the visage of the orphan.

"We all possess traits that can work together for the greater good."

The God of Peru silently passed the azure waters of the bay. Mollusks' shells of sculptural form broke the green and flowered canopy and sounded greetings. The whales stopped, and each turned a fin skyward in the salutation of the King's visit to Gastropoda. From the highest peak of the Island, a silhouetted figure of a giant snail could be seen against the clouds. "Unto Death!" The Ancient King of the snails shouted across the land, and cacophony resounded, "Unto Death!"

"They speak their allegiance well, don't they, Brother?"

"Adonis turned and was accompanied by Polyphemus and Atlas."

"Aye, my brothers. Faithful friends, unto death."

"Long have my eyes wished to behold this fair place." The mollusks' horns from the jungles of the mountain bellowed, and forming another layer of mountain height, the army of Gastropoda took their place beside the King.

"Behold! Ulysses stands at the side of Bianchi, the Ancient King, and the soldiers of Gastropoda!" The horns saluted the armies, and as all the

Before There Were Flowers

ship's eyes turned toward the heavens, the Ancient King and his soldiers slid rapidly down the slopes of Gastropoda to welcome the God of Peru and the King of Peru.

"How do giant snails move so quickly?"

"The size of Elephants and just as quick, no, Seven?" The Orphan turned to Adonis and placed his hand against the ethereal cloak.

"Why don't you call me Francis?"

Adonis turned and looked him in the eyes.

"You've chosen a name? Very good. You shall be known as Francis from this day forward."

"Prepare to move the King. I will stay with Francis." A weighted wood-colored cloak enveloped Francis and yet blew as a flag in a Seabreeze.

"Bogong?"

"Hmmm."

"What kind of king is a broken beggar?"

"Hmmm, mmmm. A king who can truly lead people."

Each mighty hand of the warriors lifted a litter woven from milkweed fibers and tattooed with symbols.

"We march with capes unfurled and the banners of the king, our queen, and The God of Peru." Morpho's eyes opened, and he touched Bogong's hand.

"Have we many gifts?"

"Two hundred, Sir, and they've been read the Terms and Conditions of their Freedom."

"All is well?"

"We have received a King's welcome, Sir. King Bianchi and his son Garbo stand at the footbridge and await your arrival."

"Ulysses?"

"He is safe, bannered, and with them."

Ulysses knelt before his sword as the king approached. The warriors stopped between the monoliths of Garbo and Bianchi's shells.

"Welcome to Gastropoda, King of Peru. The days have been long since last we saw you and your countenance much changed."

Bianchi, the ancient king, and his son Garbo leaned down their necks and wrapped an antenna around the wooden legs of Morpho.

"Bogong, take him quickly to the Apertural chambers; henceforth, we will talk in dreams."

CHAPTER 8
"The Terms and Conditions of Freedom"

"Adonis, how long will Morpho be in this cave?"

Francis stood in front of a giant shell.

"Not too long; the power of healing is great here."

"And he is held upright by this translucent substance?"

"Oh yes, it encapsulates him. It is an ancient healing technique of the snails."

Francis reached out.

"And the physicians tend to him in this pod? Diamond Back will see to him?"

"Yes, Diamond Back and the Chief of Medicine will administer care. This will be an invaluable time of education for Diamond Back. One that will undoubtedly serve us well on the ship."

Francis stared into the gel substance and could not see his reflection, but the visage of Morpho was suspended in the cocoon.

"Has he always looked this way? I mean old and...?"

"Like a caterpillar?" Francis turned to the blue Adonis.

"Yes, the wooden legs and how they toggle when he walks. The hands with the fingers bending and grasping, it's...?"

"It's a lot to see through. You're having trouble placing him in your story?"

"Why is called the King of Peru?"

"Because he is. He delivered the country from its oppressor. Read the Terms and Conditions of Freedom to its people, and they, in turn, elected him King of Peru. He returned all their gold to them, and in turn, they entrusted it back to him. This caterpillar you see is a very, very important man. To answer your question. No, he has not always looked like this. When the Captain's soul is grieving, it shows in his outward appearance. He's not like others. He cannot hide it."

"So, usually, he looks like you?"

Before There Were Flowers

"Haha, you will see it in time, Francis. Come now, I want you to meet a close friend."

"So, Garbo, by touching your shell once, our minds connect in a dream state? A place that spans time and space."

"Well, the dream space is where we problem solve, and it's where we seek wisdom from our ancestors. Ha, ha, ha, and don't forget Francis, I talk faster in this realm."

"Yes, but you do not walk faster, Garbo and yet, I must say, I am surprised that though we amble when I turn around and look from where we came, I'm amazed at how far we've come."

"Ahh, we snails are like sailing ships. Appearing to move slowly and then suddenly gone. We are actually quite rapid. You should see us in the festival of races!"

"Oh, I'd love to! Say, Garbo, would you tell me how Gastropoda was created? The snail never stopped, and Francis walked with his hand upon the giant.

"Gastropoda was made by making good choices."

"No, well, that. I mean, the Priest used to take us orphans out at night to see the stars, and there he would say," *'In the beginning, God created the Heavens and the Earth.'* "so, what I'm asking is, who is the God of Gastropoda?"

"You're asking if we have a religious tradition?"

"Yes, the Priest always said that God was perfect, and the world was made perfect. Everything that God created was perfect except man, but man was originally created to rule the world. Garbo, how can imperfection rule over perfection?"

"Hmm, Francis, now that you've been here a few days, do you see the need for a God in Gastropoda?"

"No, Garbo. Here you have peace, beauty, and love for one another."

"Hmm, aren't those the results of good choices?"

Francis stopped.

"Francis, Gastropoda is inhabited by former slaves and orphans. Each of them is read the Terms and Conditions of Freedom. Then they are given time, and when ready to immigrate to Gastropoda, they rewrite the Terms and Conditions of Freedom in their own words."

Francis walked again.

"What are these Terms and Conditions of Freedom? I want to know them, Garbo."

"Hmmm, well, tonight will be the ceremony on the beach. You will hear the Terms and Conditions in the own words of every former slave. But Francis, I warn you. Not all will choose Freedom."

"I don't understand, Garbo. These are the Terms and Conditions. What becomes of them?"

"Hmm, they stay slaves and cannot live in Gastropoda."

CHAPTER 9
"The Ceremony of Freedom"

"Adonis, there are so many here this night, such enchanted beauty abides here. The torches reflect the canopy of the palms. The new moon is witness to it."

"And look, Francis, who takes the seat of honor beside Garbo!"

"Morpho! He's alive and walking! Wait, is that a fountain of nectar?"

"Oh, dear. Yes, they will all be swimming in it before the night is over. Snails do love a good party. Incredible dancers they are. Well-traveled, well-traveled every snail."

"Bogong is with Morpho?"

"Yes, he will never leave his side. Look to the wall behind Morpho. Do you see the calligraphy there? Now, can you see it breathing?"

"Ohh, what amazement! He is completely invisible."

"Yes, ever so. Atlas and Polyphemus can be seen, but they, too, will stay with Morpho. It's for his protection."

"Here, in Gastropoda? Protection is needed?"

"Sadly, yes. This is a ceremony of freedom, but not all can see freedom in their story."

"What do you mean?"

"Hmm, to become free, a being must stop listening to the lies of others and the ones they tell themselves. You must forgive yourself, forgive others, let go of old pain, let go of anger. This is the hardest thing you will ever ask yourself to do. Some people do not have that courage, and hurt people hurt people."

"Are these the Terms and Conditions Garbo spoke of?"

"No, these are the steps that follow acknowledgment of the Terms and Conditions."

"Adonis, teacher. Would you explain to me the Terms and Conditions of Freedom? I want to know."

"Francis, when you were an orphan, you were told that you did not deserve an identity, yes?"

"That's true; I was a nobody."

"Yes, and how do you feel now?"

"I, I have a name! And that of my own choosing."

"An identity of your own, and how does that make you feel?"

"I feel respected, like I belong, and I'm wanted."

"Yes, you are wanted and respected. How do you plan on staying part of this community?"

Francis observed the festivities of the night and the seat where Morpho was guarded. "I see Atlas and know that his eyes only see truth. Therefore, I wish to always be diligent with my word. I see Bogong as the ever faithful, and therefore, I want my character to be thus. I have learned from Polyphemus to always do my best. I watched Ulysses follow his heart beyond the doubts of others and his own mind." He turned to Adonis and took his hands. "From you, Adonis, I have learned it is more important to be kind than to be thought important."

"Ahh, welcome, Francis! You have just put the Terms and Conditions of Freedom into your own words. Gastropoda will forever be your home."

CHAPTER 10
"How Were Flowers Made"

Bom, Bom, Bom. Bom, Bom. The drums of the beach ceremony started as the sparks of the bonfire perished into the night.

"Morpho, my friend. Tomorrow, we will have a council, but tonight, let's have a celebration."

"That's great advice! I have been rather weary."

"You need more balance in your wings."

"Too true, Garbo."

"Come, let's start the ceremony and then have a cup of this new nectar. Are you strong enough to stand?"

"Well, I think so."

"Very good, join me."

"To all of Gastropoda, to our Ancient King Bianchi who watches over us from the mountain, and to all the past Kings who now stand sculptured in Lungomare, I say 'Welcome'! Tonight, we will once again hold the Ceremony of Freedom. Freedom must come from within before it can ever manifest without!" Garbo's shell glowed in the firelight, and a chorus of 'Unto Death' resounded. "May every being clasp hands one with another and in our dream state put the Terms and Conditions of Freedom in your own words for all to hear. Those who do not wish to partake may be our guest this evening and trust that they are ever welcome."

The mass fell silent on the beach. Orphans sought out new mothers and fathers and held their hands. In the quiet of their minds, a thousand voices recited from the heart the terms and conditions of their individual freedom.

"Now then! There will be dancing!"

Drums, flutes, stringed instruments, twirlers of flame, whales spouting streams of effervescent water. It is as if all Gastropoda was shaking within.

"Hey, Garbo, cousin. I was just telling these fellows. Remember, when was it before the dinosaurs, I think. We went to Rio for Carnaval. Ha, ha, ha, yeah? Look at my foot. Hey, look at my foot, dis foot. You remember this? You remember this? We danced all night. Two young shells we were."

Francis, saturated in delight, mingled in and out of the Giant Snails conversing and other beings dancing.

"Listen here chaps, I used to take the big birds. No, no, yeah, yeah, the big whoopers. I'd climb aboard and say, *'Excelsior Class to London, Mate!'* You see, all my favorite pubs were there, best of nectar in the garden pubs."

"Wait, you'd take flight?"

"Oh, yeah, Francis, easy. Us Snails get around. Quite international, we are, really. No, yeah, yeah, no, the time of dinosaurs now that was luxury, express then, mate. Oh, your foothold better be good, or you need to take a ship."

"Ships?"

"Hahaha, is this your first time here, Francis? Say, question, do you relish nectar?"

"Oh, Francis, don't believe him. His shell is a bit cracked. Yeah, oh boy? Your shell about a bit cracked up there up on top?" "Aye! Use your blinkies and see your way out of here! No one is talking to you. We'll use your shell for a proper victrola one day!"

"Now, come here. I'll tell you a proper story, Francis. I took a whale, you know, like a vessel that would shuttle itself under the water all the way to New Zealand. Mind blown? Huh? Mind blown? Mine was! Amazing wonders of the deep oceans. Still friends, ole' Jumbo and me. I spent nearly two centuries there. You know, at the bottom of every glacier is a luxurious rain forest? Hundred percent, mate! Ohhh, I go back to those days in the old parts of my shell. Every little twist and turn of the trail has a waterfall of the purest water."

"Squib, Tell him about the girls!"

Francis stepped forward. "You spent two hundred years there?"

"Nearly abouts, I reckon."

"How long ago was this? When there were dinosaurs?"

"Ohh, let's see. Before there were flowers."

Francis turned serious. "Before there were flowers? What do you mean? Haven't flowers always existed?

"Oh no."

"No? Really? But what about the butterflies and moths. I mean, flowers and them were made for each other. Were they not here either?"

"Oh no, they were here, but their other half was not. Francis, it may be cruel, but we can exist in this life, even in Gastropoda, without the other half we were meant to share life with."

Francis fell quiet in the moonlight. "Squib, would you tell me how flowers were made? I think I already know."

CHAPTER II
"There is no Future, There is no Past"

"Morpho, I have something I wish to speak with you about?"

"Yes, Atlas, I know."

"You know, Captain? Sir, can you also see into the future?"

"Hahaha, Atlas, seeing someone in love doesn't take a special power. You've been mumbling to yourself and preoccupied."

"Oh, I'm sorry, my King."

"Haha, Atlas, you bring joy to my heart. Falling in love is not something you need to apologize for. However, we will need to speak to the council."

"Yes, of course, that is why I wanted to speak to you first. Captain, my heart is telling me to stay in Gastropoda."

"Let us form a circle and let this council begin. Garbo, tell us of your Father Bianchi and what of his absence?"

"To Morpho and all of this companionship. My Father Bianchi is, as you know, ancient, before the time of flowers he was. He has taken his leave to the higher place, the summit above Gastropoda. He watches over us. I will not say that he is feeble. I will say that the only words he can muster are our battle cry, 'Unto Death!' The mantle of his shell is thin, and he has retired but still finds purpose. The next time you see him, his shell will be with those of our forefathers in the Lungomare."

"Garbo, as you know, he has been a faithful companion and like a father to me."

"Thank you, Morpho. But please tell us news of the seas."

"Yes, of course. The power of the Priest is like a dark cloud covering the sea. He is recruiting all manner of creatures in his service. He has churches on the coast of Africa, collecting not only slaves but Orphans. The Wasp transports hundreds into the markets of Labadee. They sail under the banner of a crown and plunder their way across the ocean. Their Captain is not to be underestimated. If you find yourself in hand-to-hand combat with him, you must flee. Even you, Bogong. Do not engage him alone, and that is an order."

"Aye, Captain."

"We set sail for the Gold Coast in two days, but before we do, there is a matter Atlas wishes to speak of."

The circle of the council smiled and looked at each other.

"What? You don't even know what I'm about to say? Okay, I am in love. And, I see. No. I did not see this coming. For once in my life, there is no future, and there is no past. All I have to cling to is this moment of incredible joy. My heart tells me to stay in Gastropoda, yet I know my duty as a sailor to my King, my country, my ship, and you, my brothers. I cannot do both, so I am here communicating. My heart has never been so joyous and yet rent in two."

Everyone was silent around the circle, and then Morpho spoke. "Very well said, Atlas. I congratulate you on falling in love. True love is as rare as faithfulness. Those two things are only possible when we learn to give ourselves everything we need."

'Aye, aye, aye, aye.' Followed the circle.

"Something I obviously, still struggle with. Let's discover together what the absence of Atlas will mean to our mission."

"Atlas offers us so much intelligence with his eyes. He sees not only beyond the next horizon but the depths of all our memory."

Bogong spoke, "All wisdom comes from memory."

Then Garbo, "I can send the Armada to cover your wake and flanks. You can send Ulysses to fly ahead on your return."

"Yes, using the star of Gastropoda, I can find my way back here."

"Captain."

"Yes, Polyphemus. At this point in our condition and with those on board who do not accept freedom. Wouldn't the Queen protect us to her shores?"

"We sail to safety, not in the presence of safety. Remember that."

"Adonis, you've been rather quiet." Adonis, in royal colors, with jewels pooling in his eyes.

"As you know, I am no stranger to love. I walked in that garden, and the loss of it made me a slave. That's why I love Gastropoda so much. Here in the dream state, I can walk hand in hand day and night with my love. Atlas, when I was a slave, my Master did not beat me with ropes or chains. He lashed me with words. Saying, *'if you had been there. If you only would have done this. Had you stayed and not gone?'* I lived in that hell for a century of my life. During that time, I was delivered to Gastropoda three times, and three times, I denied myself freedom and returned my soul to the slave markets of Labadee. Atlas, from my point of view, there is no right or wrong decision, but there will be circumstances either way. You must follow your heart and not let the mind poison your happiness with doubt. Love commands us to do the right thing and, at times, suffer the consequences."

Garbo moved forward. "Atlas, with your King's permission. I propose that you stay here and join the armies of Gastropoda. Your service as a liaison officer will be invaluable to us all. Love will prove to be a mighty force."

'Unto Death! Unto Death!' The warriors saluted with wings unfurled and swords drawn in celebration.

CHAPTER 12
"NOT ALL CHOOSE FREEDOM"

"Good Morning, Adonis."

"And to you, Polyphemus."

"A great assembly gathers to see us off!"

"Yes, we will be on our way once this loading is completed."

"I'm surprised at how many are choosing slavery."

"Yes, yes, show them kindness, my friend. Patience and kindness."

"What were you thinking when you refused your Freedom?"

Adonis turned from the rail of the ship and looked at Polyphemus. "At that time, I was listening to a voice inside my head said that I was not good enough."

"Really, the most intelligent being I know thought he wasn't good enough for Freedom?"

"Polyphemus, I would imagine that some even hear worse things than that. The bottom line is that if you are continually choosing slavery, then you are doing so because you feel that you deserve it."

"Self-punishment?" Polyphemus observed the line of slaves reboarding the ship.

"Atlas, what do you see of our voyage to the Gold Coast."

"I see safe beyond the horizon of tomorrow. King, are you sure I should not be going with you? I…"

"Stand Atlas I salute you. We will see upon our return."

"Yes, King. Mine eyes will always be on the horizon."

"Garbo, thank you."

"The armada will sail with you to the Gold Coast. These are presents for the Queen and for you, Morpho. We give you this." And from the companionway strode a Noble beast.

"Ahh, Pegasus!"

"Yes, what is a Spaniard without a good horse?"

"Pegasus is not just a horse. Look at his mighty wings, dark as eternal night."

"Touch him, and he will be in your dream state. Unto Death!"

"Unto Death, great King."

The ancient shells of mollusks kings bellowed salutations from the arc of Lungomare, and The God of Peru plunged into the cold blue waters of a waiting sea.

CHAPTER 13
"POTENTIAL"

"Bogong, bring Francis to my Quarters."

"Aye, Sir." Francis stood in the ship's bow as if flying across the sea. "The captain wishes to see you in his quarters."

"Bogong, should I be troubled?"

"Fear not."

"Francis, take a seat. Is everyone here?" Morpho was sitting upright, his eyes and speech clear. "You are part of the ship now, and while we are underway, all aboard must do their part. You have the opportunity to become part of this crew, potentially part of this council one day."

"What is the meaning of potential?"

"Potential is a medal of honor that you have not yet earned. The process of earning it has humble beginnings. It requires a temperate will, foresight, strength, and skill. Your daily tasks aboard this vessel will teach you these things, and the council will be your instructors. You will work both in the day and in the night. You will be taught to sleep and to repair your body and mind through the dream state. Adonis will teach you strategy. Bogong will teach you tactics. Ulysses, navigation. Polyphemus will teach you every part of this ship and how to maintain it. This ship is your new country, your new home. Working with it will connect you to its dream state. Life is balanced by what we create."

"Here, Francis, you see, these are the forward compartments, the ship's stores, and this beam is the ship's keel." Francis placed his hand on the inner wall.

"I feel a vibration. Is that the sea passing by?"

"Yes, we are actually under the water here."

"Really, the sea is right on the other side of my hand?"

"Well, yes."

"And the keel serves what purpose?"

"Think of it as the backbone of a giant dinosaur."

"Where was the God of Peru made? And please do not say from good choices."

"Hahaha, well, it kind of was. It was constructed in Venice from Spanish oak. The hull is half a meter thick. Morpho watched it being built."

"Morpho, in Venice, really?"

CHAPTER 14
"Balance"

"And if we mark the noonday and bring this up to the meridian, it gives us our position. Alright, you try it."

"Ulysses, have you noticed an improvement in the captain? Look there; he's walking up and down the ship, and his beard appears to be freshly laundered."

"Ulysses, would you mind if I borrowed Francis? We've had a bit of an accident below deck."

"Adonis, there's apples covering the entire floor. How did this happen?"

"We lash every barrel down, but things happen. You know every passenger aboard the ship receives two apples a day."

"A person could eat for an entire year with all these apples."

"Really, hmm. I tell you what, Francis. Do you like sport? I wager your two apples today for all the apples in this room if; you can run across the floor without falling and touch the other bulkhead?"

"Really? The other bulkhead is not far, maybe three meters. I could possibly do that."

"You think you could run across all these apples and reach the other side without falling?"

"I think I could now. Even if I stumbled at the last moment, I reach out and touch the bulkhead before falling."

"Hmm, and the consequence would only be one day's lunch. Give it a try?"

"Yes, I'm quite anxious now!"

"Bogong, the captain, is improving rapidly. His coat is no longer tattered. His hair is trimmed, and there is the appearance of human hands."

"He fairs better with each new day. You, however, I have come to teach you tactics. It appears just in time. Has someone been abusing you?"

"Yes, Bogong, apples!"

"Who is this Apples? Is he aboard the ship?"

"Yes, yes, no. The apples that we eat. Adonis, every day of late, has wagered me all the apples on the storeroom floor if I can run across them and reach the other side without falling. So far, it has not gone as I had planned. I try each day to time it or somehow outsmart it. I've racked up quite a debt to Adonis, one I will soon never be able to pay."

"Hmm, you're why the apples have been so bruised."

"I apologize about that. I didn't think my actions would take away from your happiness."

"Francis, I understand that it would be nice to have a savings of apples. Ambition is a good thing, but may I ask you. Where would you store all those apples?"

"I haven't properly thought about that."

"Also, with all those apples, someone may wish to rob you. You would need to stand guard day and night, no doubt, to preserve your wealth?"

"Hmm, these beatings have been fruitless."

"Haha, witty."

"Francis, have you considered throwing all the apples out of the room except for two? How likely would you be able to succeed then?" Francis looked up into the eyes of Bogong.

"That is so easy!"

Adonis entered the storeroom with all the apples in the wooden cask, save two. "I wager two apples for two apples that I not only can run across this room without falling but that I can do it blindfolded."

"Hmm, I see your teacher of tactics is tired of eating bruised apples. Very good, Francis. Now that you have learned balance, you can feed yourself, pay off your debts, and still have your entire day to change the world. You are ready for capes and swords."

CHAPTER 15
"Control is Not Love"

"Captain, may I approach and meet Pegasus?"

Morpho stood on the deck, brushing the black flanks of the horse.

"Of course, Francis."

"Your shoulders are." The captain looked over. "You're feeling quite well, Sir?"

"Like a new man." Francis touched Pegasus where some would place a bridle.

"Have you always loved horses, Sir?"

"Hmm, I am a Spaniard; my Father was the treasurer of Seville. He wished for me to follow in his footsteps. The world's best teachers and all. Yet, I ran away each day to the wharf. Watched the tall ships towed in. The sailors, the soldiers. Yes, I've always loved horses. You could say it's in my blood."

"Aren't you worried that Pegasus could just run or fly away?" Their eyes met, and Francis could see a face and the broad eyes of a man looking back at him.

"Control is not love."

"Excuse me, Sir?"

"I said control is not love. Francis, did the Priest ever tell you that he loved you?"

"No, he said that God would love us if we served him. If we abided by his laws and asked for forgiveness, we could do our penance and, upon dying, live in Paradise."

"Hmm, sounds like a room full of apples to me. I do not own Pegasus. I do not bind him, tether, or promise him Paradise upon his death."

"But a ship at sea, Sir, for such a magnificent animal as this? I just see him running away in my story."

"Pegasus is in a dream state. We are all dreaming in this moment of what we perceive as justice. Let me ask you something, Francis. What if you spent each day tethering each apple to the floor so you could run across the room?"

"I can't imagine that kind of life. To tether each apple to its proper place with a ship that is constantly moving."

"And if you succeeded? Even for one day, you could cross the apples without falling as much as you want?"

"I could toil in that way every day and, in the end, be left with nothing. I would be wasting my life. Some kind of constant drama, hell."

"Many people are trying to tether apples each day, Francis. The dream state allows us to differentiate between truth and lies. Knowing thine own self allows you to tame the drama and ride it!" In one swift movement, Morpho mounted the back of Pegasus, and the great animal stood towering above the deck on two legs with wings spread. At that moment, Morpho's wooden legs were transformed into the legs of a man.

CHAPTER 16
"A CHANGED VISAGE"

"So, Ulysses, if this is our current position with calculating wind, current, the drag of our vessel… well, shouldn't we reach the Gold Coast by mid-day tomorrow?"

"By morning, I should hope! Francis, I am exceedingly proud of you. You've grown so much."

"Really, I've been too busy to notice."

"Bogong has taught you the sword?"

"Aye, and Polyphemus, the use of the cape."

"Have you taken time to take in your likeness?"

"My visage?"

"Look there in that pail of water." Francis lifted the vessel and cast his eyes into the water.

"Oh!"

"Don't worry, it's you."

"But how? I mean, I've noticed change, but."

"Gastropoda. A snail day is a year of a human's life."

"A snail day is equal to a year. Wow, they do move slowly."

"Really, look how quickly you've changed."

"And not just me. Behold, the Captain!"

Captain Morpho exited his quarters onto the deck, stepped to the side rail of the ship, and beheld the sea. Alarming silence caused him to turn and see the entire crew bowing with swords before him. "Welcome, King. It has been long since we've beheld your visage." Morpho was no longer old but made of smooth, tanned skin. His hair no longer knotted but free locks. His coat was no longer platted iron but of tailored blue with gold buttons and ribbons. His legs were no longer of twisted wood but shod in polished leather. His hands no longer root vegetables but able to clasp his sword.

"Shall I fetch a mirror for you, Sir?" Morpho looked at Polyphemus with suspect and radiant eyes.

"Flattery is appreciated but unnecessary. A handshake from each of you, a hearty good morning, and the promise of a shared cup of nectar at noon day will be sufficient."

"Aye, Captain."

"Aye."

"Aye, it is a pleasure to serve with you, Sir."

Francis took Morpho's flesh-covered hand and gazed at the simple ban of gold on his round and knuckled finger. "You have much changed, Sir."

"In your darkest hour, remind yourself that your life will look drastically different one year from now."

"Land Ho, Land Ho, Sir."

"Welcome to Africa, Francis."

CHAPTER 17
"Lions in the Dunes"

The anchors of The God of Peru ran out like cats.

"Where's the kingdom, Adonis? I thought it was on the coast, but I see nothing but miles of golden sand."

"Hahaha, Francis. This is Africa, a continent so large that you could travel for ten days inland and still be considered on the coast."

"So, when do we start our journey?"

"We wait."

"For what?"

"First to be observed and then to be invited."

"These actions are confusing."

"Francis, the Queen's Kingdom is at war. It has always been thus."

"But we serve the Queen. Morpho is her lover!"

"We are Allies of the Queen. We serve Peru and the King of Peru. An ally must approach a kingdom at war very, very carefully, or risk being destroyed. Ask yourself what would a snail do in a time like this, besides the obvious of course, drink nectar and dance the night away."

"A kingdom at war? Hmm, that's bigger than me, bigger than The God of Peru. Hmm, no. Garbo would be diligent. He would wait for directions and follow the directions."

"And so, here we are, at anchor, waiting for the Queen's directions. Dusk will be upon us soon. You'll want to turn your gaze to the dunes."

As the dusky hair of evening fell, the young man climbed into the focsle of the anchored ship.

"Bogong?"

"I'm here."

"There are shapes moving on the dunes. Things I, I think. Bogong, is that a pride of lions? They twist and turn and play as if we are not here."

"Hmm, they've been watching from the shade."

"Are they?"

"Are you asking if they are natural? Or do they serve the Queen?"

"Yes, Bogong."

"They are both. They guard the coast of the kingdom and the narrow passage inland."

"The narrow passage?"

"Yes, you will see."

"You mean we have to pass lions in a narrow space to reach the kingdom of the Queen?"

Bogong nodded as Francis rubbed his hands.

"Oh, what would a Snail do?"

CHAPTER 18
"The Greatest of Elements"

On the third anchored night, the sea swells lifted all eyes.

"Behold the red eyes of the Queen."

"And now a great host of torches precedes and follows her."

"The line of torches is steady, but the red eyes of the queen move back and forth traversing."

"How far off are they, Bogong?"

"Hmm, I know not for certain, but Morpho must be awakened."

Morpho stood with a shirt untethered.

"Captain, your glass. They've made camp behind the dunes. No flag of parle has been raised, Sir."

"Thank you, Polyphemus. Bogong, order the white flag and silence across the deck."

"Shall I lower the longboats?"

"No, assume nothing."

"Aye, Sir."

"Sir, they're lighting arrows with fire behind the dunes. Do they mean to burn our wings?"

The sea lifted and cradled the ship.

"No, Ulysses. It is our invitation."

Great numbers of flaming arrows took flight from darkness.

"The whole night has turned to fire, save a narrow path."

"Launch the boats."

"Adonis! We make landfall where lions play and guard the narrow passage."

"Hahahahaha, hahahahahah, hahahaha."

"Why are you all laughing?"

"Francis, what would a snail do?"

Francis rowed.

"Garbo would keep his hand and foot inside his shell and walk a very straight line."

"Hahahahhaha, splendid advice. I think we all shall follow your example."

"My example?"

"Captain, Sir. The beach is engulfed in flame, and there are multiple lions threatening to rip me apart. Are you asking, Sir, that I walk calmly through their midst?"

"And what's the problem, Francis?"

"Did you hear the part about the lions?"

"Hahahahahaha."

"All this laughing!"

"Oh, yes, excuse me. I'm sorry about that. No, this. This is a serious matter. Lions."

"Thank you, Sir."

"Hmm."

"Sir?"

"Oh yes. Francis, which is the greatest of elements?"

"The elements of nature, Sir? Well, Garbo says that water is the greatest."

"And why water?"

"Because if water cannot flow over or under or around something, then it will flow through it. It does not stop."

"Yes, Francis. When life blocks your path with lions, you must not stop."

"They were shackled! Tethered by anchors. Their claws whipped so close that swords of air were beating my flesh. I could see the teeth and the pink of the gums."

"Hahaha. Your path was as straight as a snail's, brother."

"Strong work, my son."

From the shadows of the night came spears. Bogong unsheathed his sword, and Ulysses drew his bow.

"Lower your arms. It's alright. I will go first."

Morpho knelt in the sand and placed his hands before him to be bound. Upright lions with shadow souls approached from the dunes.

"Are they Lions, Adonis?"

"These warriors have the souls of lions. They are equally skilled."

They wore claws over the backs of their hands, mantle pieces on their shoulders, and shields of hides strapped to forearms.

"Are they all women?"

"Yes, see how they communicate? They walk among the great beasts connected to them in their dream state."

"Amazing, another magical world of fantasy."

"Yes, but this world is not Gastropoda. This is a world at war."

Bogong turns.

"Prepare to move; we march forward."

CHAPTER 19
"The Spider Queen"

"Here, Francis, share my nectar and enjoy this shade."

"Thank you, Polyphemus."

Francis drank from a bowl.

"We've been walking for a day. How much further to the Gold City?"

"Hmm, not that far. Do you see those cliffs in the distance? Somewhere beyond them lies the city. What do you think of the country?"

"It's wonderful. Diverse, vast. The sand dunes and then oasis such as this. If my hands were not bound, I would certainly enjoy it more. It's hard to see this as a country at war."

"Yes, well, on all its borders and upon the sea. Portugal, Spain any country eager for gold is set on taking this place."

"Gold?"

"Oh yes, beneath our feet and in these streams and cliffs are significant gold deposits."

Francis looked around.

"How vast is this country?"

"Respectively speaking, it is small, but its defenses are renowned. The Queen is a master of strategy and an incredible leader of her people. Every citizen here is a warrior capable of wielding arms effectively."

"As skilled as Bogong?"

"Oh yes, you will learn much from their masters."

"How does she do it?"

"Hmm, with her brilliant mind."

"The Queen was her father's favorite child. Her brother inherited the throne, but he was no warrior or leader. He was a careless superintendent of his inheritance. The Queen stepped forward as a leader in the most desperate hour. She went to negotiate with her enemies. Being a woman, they underestimated her. They assumed she was there to give over her country, but all her port cities were blocked. They didn't even offer her a chair. So, the Queen called to the servant and asked him to kneel, and she sat upon his back. At that moment, the warrior Queen was made.

"Why didn't her enemies just take her then, at the meeting?"

"Hmmm, that's a great question and something she anticipated happening. On the same day she went to parle, she organized the coastal tribes. You see, Francis, war has little to do with swords or spears. War is all about deception."

"How so, Polyphemus?" A few tribesmen crossed over the dunes and shot arrows at the ships, taunting the iron-clad warriors, but there was a receding tide. The vessels kept having to lift anchor and move further away from the coast. As the day wore on, the few tribesmen in front of the dunes kept taunting. Finally, the soldiers had enough and were set on slaughtering the few. What did they have to fear? They had armor, but they would still need to wade through water to reach the beach, so they removed the lower parts, the metal that shod the legs. Hundreds jumped in the water, slow at first, wading to the beach and finally reaching the flood plain in the heat of the day. The ship now just as far away as the beach. The natives retreated behind the dunes, and suddenly, the heavens turned black with arrows."

"And their armor was missing from around the legs."

"Yes, those who made it to the dunes were easily overwhelmed. Exhausted from nearly mile approach. The ones who received wounds to the legs could not move, and now the tide was rising."

"They drowned?"

"Or captured."

"While the Queen was in the uficio of her enemies, she presented them a list of names of over two thousand soldiers she had captured. But the war did not stop there."

Francis finished the nectar.

"Francis, I have learned for myself in life. The things that I have chased and forced to happen have cost me severely. The best things in my life have been serendipitous."

"You mean easy, like destiny?"

"As you say it."

"Like Atlas, falling in love?"

CHAPTER 20
"Ancient Warriors"

"Bogong, does this city remind you of somewhere?"

"Aye, Herod's palace on the Mediterranean."

"Yes, of course. How the city sits on that limestone peninsula, and the slave's homes are out of sight in the cliffs beneath it. Dwellings carved into the limestone stack one on top of the other, and that massive wall around it all. We were formica living in a maze beneath the soils."

"You were both in Rome?"

"Yes, your friend Bogong was a slave, turned gladiator, from Tunisia."

"And yourself?"

"Myself? Well. A dishonored Centurion."

"Centurion? But that was…?"

"Yes, centuries ago. Ancient history. No Bogong?"

"Are you immortals?"

"Ha, no. I wouldn't say that. Our wounds heal quickly in a matter of minutes. We were born different; it just didn't manifest itself until we were a certain age and different for all of us."

"Is Morpho like you?"

"No, he does not have the same longevity. But what lacks there he makes up in brilliance."

Bogong laughed from the corner of the cell.

"Don't forget those looks!"

"Oh, yes. His looks have not hurt him a bit. Amazing how that works with him. Look at him across the way. We've marched for two days through the dunes to reach this prison, and there he stands in the middle of that yard, regal and facing the Queen's palace window."

Francis stood at the doorway of the cell. "Why does Morpho remove his sword every few minutes and wipe it with the cloth?"

"Ahh, you're very observant. It's strategy."

"Strategy for what?"

"So, he will not be challenged. He is saving his strength."

"For what?"

"Francis, do you remember when I spoke of the Queen capturing the two thousand enemy soldiers? Well, you see, her nostalgia started that day and continued to build. So many great armies led by generals marched into this land. They swore to never be defeated by a woman. The Queen started taking one soldier every night and removing him from the prison yard. Guards would escort him there into those baths. The soldier would be stripped of his clothes, and then the Queen's own attendants would bathe him in three separate baths. The soldier's body would be perfumed, and he would be given the finest of cotton robes. He would sit at table with the Queen and eat by candlelight. Then, together, they may walk in her garden, and there or inside her chambers, she'd have him. The soldier would be awakened the next morning and escorted from her chambers to a balcony stained red. Once there for all the other prisoners to see, she would take the man's life."

"This is how she met our dear Morpho. He was a sailor of Portugal and her prisoner of war. But a strange thing happened. You see, Morpho watched her every night walk past his cell, and he watched her select a man to seduce and slay. And one evening, Morpho called out and challenged the man to fight to the death for the pleasure of being seduced and then slain by the Queen."

"But she didn't slay him. He became her real lover?"

"Yes, you're right."

"But she's making him fight again?"

"Every time we return to the Gold City, this is the process. Morpho must prove and win her love again and again."

Francis sat and pondered

"Polyphemus, I have many questions about all this."

"Well, we have plenty of time."

CHAPTER 21
"THE WARTHOG"

"Wake up. Morpho has challenged."

"Who has he challenged?"

"He has challenged the Gaul."

"The Gaul! The Gaul is a giant! He's as big as two of you, Bogong."

"Hmmm." Bogong turned away pensive.

"Does he have her protection, his immortality here with her, if he is injured or speared?"

"No. He does not regain that until they union, once again."

"So, when will they fight?"

"As night approaches."

"And this is it, Adonis? There's no banners or drums, horns?"

"No, this is prison. A yard of sand and stone where he will walk out into and promptly lose his head. Quite properly."

"Seriously, Adonis?"

"Mmhmm."

"I wish, I wish, there was something I could do or say to him. Like, what would a snail do?" "I'm sorry, what would a snail do? Is that what you just said, Francis?"

"Yes, it was good advice when I heard it."

"I'm sorry, Francis, this is not snail time. This is, this is, well, this is a giant, ill-tempered Gaul who may or may not wish to be killed by a man who was a caterpillar three weeks ago. Not to mention, that he would probably rather die tomorrow morning after having been bathed by nymphs, fed a feast, and thoroughly pleasured by a Queen all night."

"Yes, yes, you're probably right; Morpho is going to get his head chopped off."

"Silence, they approach." They stood with Bogong with fingers clasped around the cell bars.

"Bogong?"

"I am here, Francis."

"Can't you intervene?"

"No."

"Why did Morpho put away his sword just now and pick up the long spear?"

"Because the Gaul is a warthog."

"A warthog?"

"Yes, he will charge Morpho."

The opponents circled inside the ring of stone and prisoners.

"The Gaul, Francis, though well-armed, cannot see very well. Watch what he does."

The Gaul positioned himself at one edge of the circle with his eyes on the sun.

"Why did he do that? Now he's completely blinded."

"Not quite; it's his technique. Watch him. He lowers himself to the sand, and there, he pushes the fine dust to a mound in front of him."

"Why?"

"He will use the dust to blind Morpho. If he can blind him and catch him in his path, then he will surely kill him."

"How do you know all this, Bogong?"

"I grew up hunting warthog; they're as dangerous as lions."

In an explosion of dust, the warthog shot forward and caught Morpho's leg, ripping through the flesh above the knee.

"Morpho is wounded!"

A crimson river flowed over the leather boots. Morpho removed his white cotton cloth from his neck and tied up the wound.

"A flesh wound, the Gaul was a second hasty. If Morpho's shadow had completely blocked the sun, he would be dead."

"But he has the spear. He could strike him at a distance when he's blinded."

"The Queen would see that as dishonorable."

"They are fighting to the death only to be killed by her tomorrow morning!"

The warthog, as if rooted in a hole, was determined to kill anything between him and the sun. "The cotton is soaked through. The Spear!"

Morpho took the spear and waved it across the sun.

"He's taunting him, but the boar will not make the same error."

Morpho steps closer to the Gaul's hole in the sand. In an explosion, the warthog charged, and in that instance, Morpho released his blue wings, blocking the entire sun. There was no space for air between the foes, and Morpho twisted like a matador. The Warthog tore through the ethereal blue wing and, in doing so, received the hidden blade of Morpho's sword in the cross of the skeleton and the spine.

CHAPTER 22
"RIPOSO"

"Why has all this been necessary?" Francis asked while folding his clothing for a pillow to lay his head upon.

"The Queen is at war, and one of her advantages as a spider is that she is unmarried, willing to kill anyone she's even been intimate with. If the other countries knew that Morpho was not only her lover but also the father of the child Luna, then we and the child would be pursued and captured and used as leverage against her."

"Where will Morpho be taken now?"

"Well, a proper bath will do him much good, but instead of being taken to the Queen's quarters, he will meet her tonight in the Eternal Fountain."

"Can it be described? Have you seen it?"

"Yes, I have seen it with my own eyes, but that was a long time ago when I was with the Legions. Adonis says he played here as a child before there was any city. He traveled here with the Great Suleyman. Is that right, brother? Before there was any city here?"

"Aye, and before there were flowers."

"This whole city is built upon artesian wells. The purest water filtered through the limestone. The Eternal Fountain is the Queen's private quarters. It's a sphere of cool spring water. Surrounded by circular walls, maybe ten meters high. Small villas, like islands, float in the water and are connected by footbridges. Fluted stone columns adorned in white cotton and the fragrance of lavender and bougainvillea. No one is there, not even servants, only the white swans and golden fish. It is the Riposo of King and Queen."

"Will we see him much?"

"Maybe from a distance. Our time here in the Golden City is used for rest. We all have our own accommodations, even you, handsome fellow. Bogong even has a wife and children."

"Wives and children." "Excuse me, wives and children?"

"You Polyphemus?"

"Me, no, I am a bachelor and a lover of many things. Listen Francis, enjoy this time of peace go explore the streets."

CHAPTER 23
"The Eternal Fountain"

Morpho awakes with the Queen's head upon his breast.

"I love you, Morpho."

"Does that mean you're not going to kill me?"

"Maybe, over time, but right now, you're too beautiful."

Morpho lolled and beheld the shadows cast by the morning sun across the body the color of a new night.

"I have loved you for ten lifetimes, and it will never be enough. Pray, tell me we can abide here and forget the world."

The white swan observed their kisses.

"Stand, Morpho, let me see your wings."

The King stretched the ethereal wings, and the room turned blue in translucent light.

"You are radiant."

"I'm a mirror reflecting you."

"Could you see how diminished I was in Gastropoda?"

"I only see the beauty within you."

She lowered her eyes.

"Yes, you much deteriorated. And it broke my heart."

"I felt lost without you."

"I am always with you in the dream state."

"Yes, I know, but my human side needed the healing that comes from your touch and reassures doubt."

She was quiet.

"How long do we have together now?"

"Not long enough."

"And Luna?"

"She's growing and blossoming."

"Is she?"

She touched his lips.

"She favors you. She has my color beneath and the radiance of wings."

"And she's...?"

"Yes, she's a mix. A being born into darkness and drawn to the light."

"She's a Moth?"

"Our Moth will lead the people well when it is her time."

"Does she know that war will be her destiny?"

"No, she is still innocent and spends her days exploring her youth."

Morpho sat down on their bed.

"I have seen her in the dream state. I wish more than anything to hold her again in my arms."

CHAPTER 24
"A Friend of Garbo's"

Morpho awakes with the Queen's head upon his breast.
"I love you, Morpho."
"Does that mean you're not going to kill me?"
"Maybe, over time, but right now, you're too beautiful."
Morpho rolled and beheld the shadows cast by the morning sun across the body the color of a new night.
"I have loved you for ten lifetimes, and it will never be enough. Pray, tell me we can abide here and forget the world."
The white swan observed their kisses.
"Stand, Morpho, let me see your wings."
The King stretched the ethereal wings, and the room turned blue in translucent light.

"You are radiant."
"I'm a mirror reflecting you."
"Could you see how diminished I was in Gastropoda?"
"I only see the beauty within you."
She lowered her eyes.
"Yes, you much deteriorated. And it broke my heart."
"I felt lost without you."
"I am always with you in the dream state."
"Yes, I know, but my human side needed the healing that comes from your touch and reassures doubt."
She was quiet.
"How long do we have together now?"
"Not long enough."
"And Luna?"
"She's growing and blossoming."

"Is she?"

She touched his lips.

"She favors you. She has my color beneath and the radiance of wings."

"And she's...?"

"Yes, she's a mix. A being born into darkness and drawn to the light."

"She's a Moth?"

"Our Moth will lead the people well when it is her time."

"Does she know that war will be her destiny?"

"No, she is still innocent and spends her days exploring her youth."

Morpho sat down on their bed.

"I have seen her in the dream state. I wish more than anything to hold her again in my arms."

CHAPTER 25
"The Language of Every Heart"

Adonis wields Arabian steel with talismans and engravings. "And that, Francis, is how you take the sword of your enemy. Now, you try." Francis engages the heavy blade.

"No, not quite. Bogong?"

"I am here."

"Would you mind working with Francis? I want to see his footwork." The blades cross on the practice ground.

"Alright, Francis. I want you to enter the dream state while fighting."

"You mean begin dreaming in battle?"

"Precisely. It's just the five of us. Talk to us about what's on your mind. Again, Bogong, attack."

"I have questions. I don't understand the King and Queen's relationship."

"Oh, you wish to talk about relationships? Wait one moment, Polyphemus?" Francis relaxes, though sparring with Bogong.

"Polyphemus, I don't understand how the Queen could take a different lover every night and still be in love with Morpho. And vice versa, how could Morpho love her knowing that she...? Well, I don't understand because he takes no other that I have seen. Does he?"

"No, we are always with him, and no, he doesn't. Furthermore, if he did, the Queen would kill him. Right, Bogong?"

"Indeed, he'd be dead."

"Well, I don't think that would work for me."

"Hmmm, I see. Francis, do you remember the beach ceremony on Gastropoda where all the former slaves put the Terms and Conditions of Freedom in their own words?" Bogong changed forms. "If all the slaves were given parchment and told to copy a set list of Terms and Conditions, would it be the same?" Francis advanced.

"No, it wouldn't be the same. It wouldn't be."

"Real?"

"Genuine."

"Ahhh, yes, genuine."

"You know, in Italy, we have a word for couples, coppia. Its meaning is a partner."

"I'm listening." Francis twisted and struck Bogong's flank.

"Well, there are two types of partners in the world: those who prefer many lovers and those who prefer one."

"Explain that more, please. Bogong, are you out of breath?"

"Well, for instance. Bogong here has many wives and many children." Bogong begins to speak.

"And they have many husbands and other children."

"That doesn't bother you, Bogong?"

"Bother me? It has nothing to do with me. Their bodies and minds are gifts to me. Gifts are to be cherished, not owned or enslaved."

"And you, Ulysses, what is your take on love?" Ulysses joins the fight.

"I am open to love and would like to have a life partner, but I am not open to drama or disrespect. For this reason, I am single. In the absence, I have focused on the half of the relationship I am responsible for – my half." Francis took up a long spear and Ulysses continued. "I have, for the first time, begun to give myself all that I need. In doing so, every new day is a dreamy romance. This doesn't mean I would refuse the nectar of love, but if it is not love, then I do not have to be there."

"Polyphemus, are you married?"

"No, no, no, no, Francis, I am a bachelor and a lover of many things. I consider myself an artist. In doing so, I have the liberty to share and compare my art. I am not meant to be given to one type of wine. Why not talk with Adonis?"

Francis took the sword of Bogong. "Adonis, what do you know of true love?"

"I once was alone. Single, not much different than Polyphemus save one enchanted evening. I saw her first adorned in red. She turned and looked immediately into my eyes. We stayed up the whole night talking under the new moon. She is my best friend and Alpha and Omega to this day. She died in my arms, and I, hah, I was helpless and could not save her." The match stopped, and Adonis wept. "You see, Francis, in that time we had together, she gave me enough love for a hundred lifetimes. I wait for her to be reborn, and I have all I need in that hope."

Bogong renews the attack. "So, does each of you feel you're experiencing true love?"

"Francis, Freedom is another word for love, and every person must describe love in their own words." So, how do you fine-tune your balance and not hurt hearts?"

"What have you been doing this whole time?" Francis realized he was still in a fight.

"I have been listening, asking questions, and communicating. I have experienced a flow of emotions that resounds in truth. Is truth the language of every heart?" Francis took the sword of Bogong.

CHAPTER 26
"Two Hearts Collide"

Two hands reach for a stone, and two hearts collide. "Oh!"

"Oh, my! I'm sorry I did not see you there." Luna and Francis fall backward, having struck heads.

"I was reaching down for this heart-shaped piece of quartz."

"Me too."

"But I feel like I've run into the chest of Bogong."

"You mean Bogong the warrior?"

"No, I mean Bogong the father."

"What are you doing on my path? I thought no one else traveled this way."

"Your path? I found this a long time ago, and I, too, thought no one else traveled here. And now we've reached together for this trinket of happiness. It reflects your color well in this light." She looked into his eyes.

"You should have it."

"Why?"

"Oh, Pegasus is here."

"And he knows you. How?"

"We met in Gastropoda, the land of the Giant Snails. Would you mind if we walked together along these paths of ours?"

"I would like that." Pegasus follows the two beating hearts.

"So, what you're saying is that if either of us was given this stone of happiness to carry for the other, it would become a burden?"

"Possibly. You see, Garbo once said to me. Happiness is a light that all were given to illuminate their own darkness. And if you give your happiness to someone else, then you will be left in a darkness of resentment. I know this is just a stone."

"No, Francis, this is not just a stone. It is a heart-shaped stone we both found unexpectedly on our paths and reached for."

"What should we do?"

"I suggest," she lifted and pecked his lips, "that we leave this stone as a marker of where our journey began and then meet each day to play together."

CHAPTER 27
"Theridiidae"

Moonlight ripples across the sphere of the Eternal Fountain. "I want to see you in this light."

The Queen loosens Morpho's robe and leads him to water.

"Theridiidae." She kisses his chest, and his hands fall from her shoulders. He pulls her tight against him.

"The water turns to diamonds as it touches you."

"Chase me, then." And as one swan chases another, they played.

"We have to talk about the Seventh Orphan."

"He's taken the name of Francis."

"I'd prefer him not to have a name."

"Theridiidae, he is good, not evil."

"The Priest raised him, and I'm not sure you can get that evil entirely out of you. He has a purpose, and I will make sure it is for the benefit of my people."

"If you force his power to the surface, Theridiidae, you may create a creature that you then may have to destroy. Why not wait? He will go back to the sea on The God of Peru. Give him time. Invest in him." She disappeared shadow into shadow. "Are you hearing me? Do not ignore my council, answer me!"

A finger of the night appeared bent and touched the base of the neck.

"You do not command me." Morpho plunged into the darkness and found it vacant.

Later, rubies adorned the ebony flesh of the Queen. "Would you come to our bed?"

Morpho sits on the bed and touches her. "What are your fears, Theridiidae?"

"I fear they are forming an armada to sail against this land. If they find the Seventh Orphan, they will use his power to divide this country and sail through the center of it. And yet, with him here, he could unknowingly render this city asunder." Morpho's hand laid flat against her back.

"So, you fear it is time for us to go."

"No, I fear that the Salt and Swan Lords have betrayed us."

CHAPTER 28
"The Salt Lord"

"Ulysses, would you tell the council what you've told me."

"The God of Peru lies surrounded by grass, sea grass, and soon Rocha will embed her keel."

"How is this possible, Ulysses?"

"Polyphemus, the Salt Lord, has peculiar powers over the bottom of the sea. Salt, sand, grass, creatures that abide there."

"So, we attack him." Morpho steps forward.

"We cannot attack him by land. His kingdom, his 'Terra Firma,' is a mass of floating barges in shallow water. It moves at a distance with the tides offering protection."

"Captain."

"Yes, Adonis."

"Are our wings strong enough to lift The God of Peru from her peril and deliver her to the sea?" "Possibly, but Atlas and Diamond Back are not here, and if we were successful in lifting her, then the Salt Lord's armada of swift boats are waiting for us. Small boats, a forward gun, nothing more lethal to a ship."

"Can we mask the ship with our wings?"

"They know the ship's position, and if the Swan Lord has betrayed us, then they know our tactics of masking and disappearing."

"Reflecting the sun, Sir?"

"Their eyes have long been accustomed to it. They have keen vision."

"Are we without a plan?"

"No. The Queen travels to the border lands to seek the vision of the Heron and Fish. We will move tomorrow to the dunes and wait for Diamond Back to rejoin us from the West. Our course of action will be determined through reconnaissance. Take today to square your debts and embrace your loved ones."

"Father! Bogong, Polyphemus, and Francis?" They all turned to see

Luna in her radiance. Thin lines of colorati sculpted her visage.

"Luna, darling, I didn't know you knew of this place. Wait, how do you know Francis?" "Pegasus, insist we come here every day. He kneels and faces the east, and if in a dream state, he prays to loved ones beyond this horizon.

"Pegasus is praying to the East?"

"Tesoro mio." Polyphemus embraces Luna and kisses her head.

"Bogong, you promised me, tandoori."

"Yes, I am impeccable with my word. This evening, I shall prepare the feast." They embrace, and then Luna intertwines her hands with Francis's like olive branches twisted by volcanic wind.

"Pegasus, Pegasus, Pegasus, is our redeemer. We meet tomorrow in the dunes."

CHAPTER 29
"The Foundation of Love"

"Excuse me, Francis. Luna, may we have a word together, alone Darling? Just a moment?"

Pegasus turned and followed his masters. "Luna, you seem to know Francis quite well."

"Of course, Father, I tell you and Mother about our adventures in the great forest every evening."

"You've spoken of the snail friend of Garbo's, not this young man."

"Of course, I have, Father. Maybe you assumed Francis was a snail, but no, he doesn't strike me as one. What is he do you think? Something majestic, no doubt?" She turned to Morpho.

"Majestic? I don't, uh, I don't, well, I don't know about all that."

"Does your mother know that the friend in the forest is a young man and not a snail?"

"The Queen Theridiidae? She is always busy or gone. I've tried to speak with her about Francis of late, but I'm not sure she hears me. You, too, Father, are distant in your work. Which brings a question? When I reach maturity, will I always be gone and leave my children alone?" Morpho looks away in shame.

"Your Mother and I are trying to change the world into a better place for you." Luna turns to wipe tears away.

"And I believe that is true, Father. Francis often speaks of balance." Morpho joins her.

"Darling, Francis may not be the person you think he is."

"Hmm? You're trying to scare me away from love?"

"No, Darling, I'm trying to protect you."

"Do not patronize me with 'Darling', and I do not wish to be protected from Francis! He gives me something neither you nor Mother, Bogong, or Polyphemus can give me, and I don't expect you to understand. He does not lead me or follow me, but he walks beside me as an equal. He does not try and fix my problems but simply listens. Bogong's wives tell me. Mutual respect is the foundation of love."

"You've been going to Bogong's wives for advice on love?"

"Come, Pegasus." The horse embraced Luna's hand. "Francis, I'm ready; we shouldn't be late for Bogong's tandoori!"

CHAPTER 30
"Diamond Back"

"How fair thee?"

"Bogong?"

"Follow my steps; I will lead through the dunes." Diamond Back follows the shadow's footprints.

"How are your supplies? Was the trip worth it?"

"Oh yes, Captain, though I brought back compounds, concentrated forms, you see. Something to mix and expand."

"I see. You approached from a different direction."

"Yes, yes, you're correct, Sir. There are strange footprints about, Sir."

"In what manner?"

"This, you see, here, Sir." The stick was used and discarded.

"Bogong, the Swan Lord, moves to our flank. Send Ulysses."

"Aye, Sir."

"Do you remember the ancient city of Cumae when it was attacked by Etruscans? They sailed the ship through the cave to the inner harbor. When the Etruscans followed, they fired down upon them from the cliffs."

"Well, yes, Captain. The tide rose and trapped them; it was fish in a barrel, but we do not have the armies of Gastropoda here."

"Nay, Captain, he's right. We have no allies, well, save one."

"That's out of the question."

"But Sir, if I may. The God of Peru is surrounded, no less by the Salt Lord, who doubtless is waiting only for us to attempt a rescue and then set fire not only to her mast but our wings. And the Swan Lord moves upon our flank, and if we tarry in nonaction, we too will be cut off."

"Yes, I know. The Queen orders us to wait until vision is rendered from the Oracles, but we are pushed to the limitations."

"Sir, forgive me, but is their vision steadfast? Isn't it proffered with bones of poultry and swine, cast and rent lots of riddles?"

Before There Were Flowers

"Hmm, the Heron and the Fish." Morpho crossed his arms and looked down.

"I cannot go to Felionia. Yes, her armies are what we need, but, well, in this scenario, it may cause war from within. That may be exactly what our enemies wish upon us, self-destruction."

"What of the armies of the Golden City?"

"Too few, I'm afraid. The Old Guard travels with the Queen for her protection to the far north, and the regiments in place patrol the walls and the great forest. The treaty between the Queen and The Princess of Cats is understood but never spoken of. That is why it is best if a proxy goes in my stead to ask for reinforcements. Who will go?" Morpho looked at each face. "Bogong?" The darkness in the night shifted.

"I cannot."

"But Bogong, you have many wives to see, and Felionia and her feline warriors will…"

"One can have many wives and still not be seen." The gladiator paused. "Felionia truly sees me." The others chuckled.

"Polyphemus? Will you take up the mantle?"

"My King, this is surely the way I do wish to perish, in the arms of such delightful creatures, but My lord, I do not wish to die today." He sheathed his sword.

"Ulysses?"

"Captain, I have flown many times into danger but into a den of such enchanters; well, Captain, they banter at my wings, you see, but if they could be tamed."

"No, never; please, Captain, leave them as they are, untamed." Polyphemus stepped back into the night.

"Adonis?"

"My King, it's quite impossible. I can only see that it is you that must go."

"What's the matter, brother? Not enough tuna?"

"Ha-ha, humor. I once heard Bogong try to make a joke. No, it's not a matter of sufficiency; it's much worse. We were born under the same star sign."

"Oh, dear God, man. Salvation has no mercy upon you. Forever Friends? Oh, by Christ!"

"Yes, it is a rather cruel form of punishment. Felionia has drawn a rather invisible line between her body and mine. My heart scours the perimeter for weaknesses and yet defies the attempts by saying, *'You'll never know what your friendship has meant to me.'*

"Oh God, I'd fall on my sword for mercy."

"I'd tear off my own wings." Bogong looks to the heavens.

"An opaque destiny."

CHAPTER 31
"The Princess of Cats"

"Who is this Princess of Cats, and why must Morpho go to her through the dunes alone?" Laughter crowds the air.

"Is she really that powerful and enchanting?" Laughter murmurs to itself.

"Come now, please. Polyphemus? In this firelight, you all look devilish and mad. What makes this Felionia so enchanting?"

"Confidence."

"Aye, confidence she propels it like a javelin."

"Is she a God?"

"Oh, God, yes."

"Is she fairer than others? Taller? More, brilliant?" For once, they turned serious.

"No, no, there are fairer, yes. There are taller, no doubt, but?"

"But what? Can you tell me?" Adonis looked at him in the firelight.

"She is Queen. And she moves as if treading a carpet unseen."

"Confidence? Is that what it means? What is her Kingdom?"

"Oh, every tin of fish."

"Do you remember Boaz?"

"Haha, yes. You can save a King from everything except himself. He met Felionia and then turned himself to pasture for ten years. He lived in the Campagna with oxen, the King of Babylon, feeding and dunging among cattle."

"Born under the same star sign."

"Oh! You're right! I never thought of that. Forever friends turned him mad!"

"Aye, love is the greatest of sickness and yet the very antidote to it."

"How have you done it Adonis, stayed sane?"

"Oh, ha-ha, have I?" He peered into the far night. "I just have lately resigned myself that it's never going to happen again, for me. It's just not in the stars. Or maybe that star you know has just burned out now. Like, I caught the tail end of its light those last few days. And where love once was held for me and where I hoped it would be again but now, I'm realizing that there's nothing there to reflect love's light to me."

"Oh, don't say that."

"No, no, I mean. I haven't given up hope entirely, just on my mind."

"It's sounds that way."

"Do you remember Mary Magdalen?" Polyphemus leaned forward into the light.

"You're talking about the true artist who fell in love with Christ?"

"Indeed, Jesus was the fellow. Remember all that trouble?"

"Of course, hard not to."

"In Germania, many Centurions would sit at night and proclaim that when they returned home, they'd prove their salt and ask Mary to wed. Being honest, I, too, would lay in my tent at night and think of life with her. Funny, a soldier in the midst of war and bloodshed and yet can be brought to tears over loneliness. Wanting to be comforted and touched, nurtured even. No other woman could make you feel the way Mary did. With just a few words, the heart took wing. Men would say, 'Worth her salt that Mary.' Stand would we in front of that house, others near or purring near us, and yet we abided for the audience of Mary. Huh, Centurions laden in armor and leather strapping, crimson scarfs. Showing athleticism over boasting to her of our chariots, wielding our swords and then comes Jesus in his wood maker sandals. He stops at Mary's and says to hear in that soft voice. *'How are you feeling today?'* That's what he said. Not of chariots, gladiators, or pounds of salt, but *'how are you feeling today?'* We were dumbfounded and doubtless repeated it like fools. *'How are you feeling today?'* And the sweetest of words would pass her lips. *'cosi, cosi.'* Oh, we hated him. I mean, don't get me wrong, he was a nice fellow, misunderstood, yes, of course. But, well. We would jest with him. Say, what is your profession? I can't tell from your untethered hair and white cotton robes. He'd speak, and we'd cock our ears and say louder! Again, never frustrated, the response came. *'I'm an artist.'* Fisher of men, I'd say. Truly, painfully, fisher of women. Mary's gaze fell upon him. Hmmm. He would be gone for a few days, and Mary would ask *'where hast thou been?'* He'd say something like. *'I took my boat upon the sea and watched the stars all night.'* Like candles, Mary's eyes illuminated, and she'd return 'pensando a te.' She'd sit and move his hair behind his ear and feed him figs, that purple love fruit, irresistible. We were all witness to him stealing her away. Then he wrote the book and healed the sick, and I, too, remember when he fed the five thousand. Mary would say, *'read to me more of your book.'* And he would touch her hand and say. *'I'm becoming more conflicted with its end.'* And she'd return. *'Tell me again how it's written.'* He'd sit and thumb its empty pages and say. *'You, see Mary, my life story is written with love.'* He fished her heart to him with words. Bound herself to him with truth."

"Was he God?" Francis asked.

"Of course, he was. Who else deserved her love?" He breathed deeply. "It was a shame; I mean, don't get me wrong. We all hated him for stealing her away. Even Herod fancied Mary even more than his slave boy."

"Polyphemus, did you crucify Christ?"

"Oh, no, Francis, God no, of course not. All I did was stab him."

"What? You stabbed Christ?"

"Oh, yeah, I've stabbed many men, quite easy."

"You stabbed Christ?"

"He was dead, already. It's no big deal. I mean, it bothered me, yes, for a while, but then I forgave myself for it."

"You forgave yourself for stabbing a man? You forgave your own self?"

"Yes, I highly recommend it. Well, Adonis helped me realize and understand that it was, in some way it was God's will and that, in the larger scheme of the world, it was destiny, and therefore, I had no real control over the situation. Made me feel a lot better."

"Adonis helped you rationalize your stabbing Christ?"

"Exactly, my friend Adonis."

"Listen, Francis, Jesus was a great prophet. I learned much from his teachings and still remember, sourly of course, the lessons he taught me about love." Polyphemus turned to Francis and wrote in the sand. "You see here this name, Caesar? Do you know what that name means?"

"No, I do not."

"When the Senate selects a new ruler of Rome he is given the name Caesar and is thought in that moment to become a god. The name Caesar means son of God. You see, just as Jesus used words to fish Mary's heart to his. His ego used words to betray his truthful message. When he entered Jerusalem, he claimed to be the Son of God. Francis, Rome could only have one Caesar."

"So, is this why you've always been a Bachelor? Because Jesus won Mary's affection?" Polyphemus thought.

"I think it has to do more with the last thing I ever heard him say. She came with others to Golgotha to remove his body. I umm, I don't know if you've ever witnessed a crucifixion, but uhm, God could not survive that much less a man. His flesh was ripped and bones where showing. His legs broken and of course the nasty wound in his side that I gave him." Polyphemus stopped. "I, I watched her as they laid his cross and body down. We all did. All of us that at one time or another Mary had given her body too. It was like we didn't exist. Like we were dust in the air, undetectable. I mean that her self- judgement was undetectable. She was not embarrassed that we had all known her, and yet here she was professing her true love for this man. You see, that's what gets me. In Jesus's eyes, he was the one with greater shame. She had given her body to men and women in that community and sure people heaped scorn and shame upon her, but Jesus had given his body to the whole world. To every man and to every woman and for her to love him unconditionally without judgement of his future or past was the love that he wrote his story with."

"She knelt over him. Not going to his head, with the thorns or the hands that had been nailed or the legs broken, but she went to his feet and there hovered. She had no water for washing save her tears. She had no cloth save her own hair. She wept and washed his feet and she whispered, *'When I cannot look at you, I look at your feet. Hard and boney yet I love them. Because they walked on Earth, and upon water and across the wind of time until they found me.'*

CHAPTER 32
"The Sacred Ornaments"

"Would you like for me to go, Sir? To this Princess of Cats?" All eyes turned to Francis, then lifted to Morpho. "I may be immune to her?" Morpho looked for direction.

"Youth may spare him; his innocence may spare him."

"We are ancient, maybe ancient fools, in this way, Sir. He does not have wings, yet." Francis turned his head at this.

"Adonis, may I see you privately?"

"Captain, why are we here?"

"I want your council."

"No, Captain, I meant, why are we in this position? Here, in the dunes, with The God of Peru slowly being surrounded by the powers of the Salt Lord."

"Are you questioning my leadership?"

"No, but I think you are."

"Then you'd be right. Everything rises and falls on leadership. These perils have accumulated quickly. Have I been overconfident? Did I leave the ship unprotected?" Adonis only listened. "Why did I bring the Seventh Orphan within the walls of the Golden City? Am I so careless that my enemies have been sitting back and waiting for me to destroy us?" Morpho leans over a basin and investigates his reflection. "I never should have left Atlas in Gastropoda. We are blind without him."

"Again."

"Again, what?"

"Ask yourself why and keep asking yourself why." Adonis leans over and peers eye-to-eye with Morpho.

"You will find that the fault is not in your leadership. We have been betrayed. We need to ask why the Salt and Swan Lords betrayed us. Power, greed, fear? We know ourselves, Captain. We need to seek to know our enemies."

"The Swans have been the guardians of the eternal fountain for centuries."

"And what is it they have heard and reported?"

"Something from the Queen or Me."

"Or Luna?"

"Our Daughter!"

"The future Queen of the Golden City." Morpho peered deep into the royal eyes of Adonis.

"They don't want The God of Peru. They wanted to distract us and leave her unprotected. Oh God! Send Ulysses with Pegasus to the city at once! Have them bear her to us immediately!"

"Can you reach the Queen through the dream state to warn her?"

"No, not when she seeks the vision of the Oracles. They feed her heart fruit and mine the subconsciousness. Runners will be sent to the Old Guard."

Ulysses and Pegasus are commanded and take flight. "Morpho, they speed away. Our enemy is large. Not just the Swan and Salt Lords but Portugal, Spain, and now this East India Trading Company."

"What are you saying, Adonis? That I must prepare myself to lose something, to lose my daughter?"

"They have been clever, yes. I think we should use the Sacred Ornaments, Sir."

"The Sacred Ornaments. The shells of adornment and the bark shields? You fear greatly, Adonis."

"What I feel is our house is built upon sand."

"To invoke the Sacred Ornaments, Adonis, would that be admitting failure?"

"Captain, the Sacred Ornaments were created for times like these. To not invoke them would be pride."

CHAPTER 33
"Simplicity of Innocence"

"Bogong?"

"I'm here, Captain."

"Would you bring me the Sacred Ornaments, please?" Morpho sat alone with a delicate brush in his hand.

"As you commanded, Sir."

"What?"

"The box of plum heart, the Sacred Ornaments, Sir." Morpho looked at the box and then touched the bristles of the brush with his fingertips.

"Sit with me and be seen." Bogong moved slowly and became visible.

"This brush itself is a Sacred Ornament. A talisman to me. When Luna was a child, you know, maybe three or four years old, we spent every day in the garden of the Eternal Fountain. Just being a family. No cares, no worries, you just silently basking in the light. Luna would start each day on her knees with some bit of parchment before her. Lines, shapes, cats. Whatever entered her mind, she drew on the page. Black and white, you see. The simplicity of innocence. Her Mother. Well, she never knew her mother was a queen. Luna never knew any caretaker, save us. She didn't know of the kingdom or war, peril, or danger. Just this brush and her imagination. Her mother's hand placed on hers guiding the lines at times. Writing out at times *cat, dog, snail, spider.* One day, with this brush, she drew a family portrait. Us in the garden. Me not with wings, or cape or sword. Her mother not with fine armament or with her guards but just us. Her mother's loving arms around her. That day, Luna told her mother that the picture needed more. Theridiidae brought her and the portrait to me. *'What more does it need?'* she said. Theridiidae sat upon me and touched the back of my neck. *'Is she asking for a sibling?'* Our heads twisted like retrievers fascinated with the thought of another blessing. Then Luna reached out and touched her mother's skin. Her little finger rubbed the pigment. Then she touched her own hands and then slowly she pointed into my eyes. Her portrait was incomplete because her imagination drew no longer in black and white but in color. Her mother knew instantly. She took the tender hand and formed the child's fingers around this bit of sprig and she touched the bristles to the palette of her own skin and Luna painted her in lovely shades. Next, the child ran the horsehair over my eyes, and their color clung to these bristles and so she painted. With this brush she touched flowers, and wings of birds, and ripe fruit and butterflies. The child and her mother touched all living things, and they became all loving things. And everything good in the world she made beautiful."

Before There Were Flowers

CHAPTER 34
"A Deep Keeled Vessel"

"Ulysses! You've returned. Where is she?" Morpho's hands embrace the cheeks of the flyer, but his eyes drop.

"Captain, she is not in the Golden City. No one knows where she is." Morpho's hands drop. "Her tracks, though. We found her tracks alone, leading through the great wood and…"

"Out of the safe places, you mean?"

"Yes, my King."

"How far?"

"My King, she reached the open sands, and there, my lord, her tracks end, and another begins. Like this."

"The Swans have her?"

"I can't say that for true, Sir."

"Why not?"

"It's a Swan track, not an accompaniment. Pegasus is still following it."

"A horse?"

"A warrior, Sir, in a different form."

Morpho turns away. "There's more, Sir. As I flew, masked by the blue sky, I saw troops of men in armor disembarking ships and marching into the dunes. Sir, time is of the essence, and we cannot abide here. They are assembling machines that throw mighty nets into the sky. Cannons chained to beast are being dragged forward, and there is a Man of War, a ship of blackness coursing and commanding offshore in the place of forty fathoms." Morpho turns.

"A deep-keeled vessel with black sails?"

"Aye, Sir."

"The Second Orphan."

"How many Orphans are there?"

"So far, Seven." Morpho draws the short sword. "Assemble the council and prepare the assembly to move."

Before There Were Flowers

CHAPTER 35
"We Gather Faith"

The stoic council assembles in the candlelighted tent of Morpho. "Bogong, the box of Sacred Ornaments." The box of plum heartwood opened. Lines of polished spiraled shells appear lying in velvet, and around the box lay shields of bark wood.

"Before there were flowers, there was only the power of the Word. The Word shaped the World. There were no swords or spears or ships of war. There were no countries to be at war. There was no buying or selling of sugar or slaves. No beast or mankind, only beings. We walked together in Gastropoda before there were flowers, and we knew all things that existed, and yet we knew there were things that would one day exist. We couldn't imagine these beautiful things, yet inside every beating heart, there lay hope that they would be born one day. We were made for flowers, but flowers had not yet been created. Hope sustained us, and we shared hope using the power of the Word. In that time when there was no flower nectar, we suckled at the bark breast of these Sacred trees." Morpho lifted one of the bark shields, and as he did, lantern light illuminated the calligraphy of tattoos from his cape and sword, shown blue in the night. The veins of the bark shield glowed, and ancient words of powerful names could be seen, and the outline of mighty wings appeared.

He passed a torch over the polished shells, and the hues of green and blue gold words were seen from within. The warriors unsheathed their swords and crossed their blades, and the power of the gold words leaped from the shells to the steel, and calligraphy could be seen growing as vines of courage to each beings' breast and forming the tattooed lines of wings. Morpho laid down the shield, and as he did, branches sprouted from it, leafed and bloomed. He picked up one of the spiraled shells and cupped it like a beating heart in both hands. Strands of leather fell from it. He walked to Bogong, and the giant lowered his head. The King placed the Sacred Ornament around his neck as a spiraled radiance in the center of the golden-worded wings. His arms alite with gold calligraphy, and they danced with the names written upon his cape. Then to Adonis, and likewise, Polyphemus and Ulysses. Francis was not adorned, nor was

Diamond Back present. The Beings stood glowing in blues and golds, and the lanterns went out not in jealousy but in reverence of the Word.

"This light will serve as a beacon to all our Allies: the armies of Gastropoda, the legions of the Golden Kingdom, all the past leaders of war and peace, to all those The God of Peru has delivered from the slave ships to the shores of Lungomare. When we practice this ritual, we gather faith."

Bogong steps forward and picks up one of the bark shields. It grows in the light to fight his size, and branches grow to fit his mighty forearm. "Prepare to move with night. We fly to The God of Peru."

Before There Were Flowers

CHAPTER 36
"Practice Our Movements"

Morpho unrolls a map. "This is the Gold Coast, where The God of Peru has set at anchor. The Salt Lord's barge kingdom lies outside the harbor. He blocks the passage to open water and patrols it with small boats. A few kilometers to the north are the Orecchio's, a series of limestone caves. Still, this one, once inhabited by the soldiers of Greece coming back from Troy, opens up to a lagoon, and hidden in the cliff face is the narrow passage of the underground river that flows from the Golden City. The plan is to board the ship in the cover of darkness. Quietly, we will ready her, and when the tide recedes before sunrise, we will drift towards the inlet and the barge kingdom. We will be in close combat; therefore, the gun carriages will be removed under every cannon and loaded with chains. Their eyes are keen and will see the ship moving before first light. We will light arrows with fire, and as the land breeze out to sea, we will set fire to the barge kingdom and let the wind scatter it. We will then fire our canon into the barge city and open the passage before us. This is where the Sacred shields will defend us. The shields will be set fast into the rail of the ship. The small boats will undoubtedly attack us like bees. Polyphemus, you will do what you do best here." Polyphemus drew two long knives.

"Once clear of the barge kingdom, we will just be entering danger. There is a deep-keeled Man of War just offshore. The outgoing tide will keep him from coming closer, but we will be within range of its long guns. Though far away, the captain of that vessel has a way of seeing. He will not just target the God of Peru. He will target the Sacred shells that cover every heart. Bogong, though I know it will be difficult, you must stay connected to the ship. Give us your invisibility, fight with hand, but save us from his sight with your other. Diamond Back? Where is Diamond Back?"

"I'm here Sir, just getting topside now."

"Diamond Back, you must fight with us on deck."

"But Captain, now, I'm just a simple sailor. A man of medical experience not of these implements of, of, war."

"If Francis can certainly stand shoulder to shoulder with us and fight, then you can. When this is over, you will have much to do in your surgery, and we will not forget you then." Morpho turns back to the council. "We will only move into open water as long as the tide will carry us. When it changes, we will drift back and enter the narrow passage of the cave harbor."

"That's sure death, Sir."

"Yes, and so the Salt Lord will think us an easy prize." He will enter through the cave in his small ships, ready to fire upon us and sink us, but we will be invisible. The canons will be leveled and loaded with fragment grenades and chains. No one can survive that. Now then, let's lay the ship's perimeter out in the sand and practice our movements."

CHAPTER 37
"THE EVIL EYE"

"Captain, two suns are rising in the east."

"No, Bogong, one is the Evil Eye. Quick with the shields and light the arrows."

When the Sacred bark shields met the hull of the ship, a great noise, like thunder, could be heard.

"Adonis, Adonis, the shields are growing branches!"

"Stand back, Francis. They're incapsulating the ship. Some are oars propelling us!"

"They are intertwining like the massive trees in the jungle Gastropoda. Could it be?"

"We called out, and they heard us! Light your arrows, Francis."

Bogong stood with a mighty hand against the mast, the Sacred shell glowing blue gold in his breast, and his sword raised in threat to the evil eye.

"Fire!" At that moment, a light more brilliant than the rising sun domed from the ship, and the arrows carried with the land breeze found their marks on the Salt Lord's Kingdom.

"They are in disarray, Sir."

"Stand by to fire the cannons." From the iris of the Evil Eye flew fiery harpoons across the sky. "He will not miss again."

The mercenaries of the Salt Lord lunged from the fiery barges toward the ship, and the branches encapsulating the vessel swatted them away like flies. "The ship is protecting itself!"

"She does that, Francis!"

Having seen the fiery dart of the Evil Eye, Bogong embraced the mast like a lover and closed his eyes, and all was darkness. The marauders flung back into the burning sea as if lifted by the wind. They drifted into the shallow havens of the sea.

"Look fast, men, and do not waver. The Salt Lord's men are boarding boats."

"Adonis."

"Yes, Francis."

"There's too many to number."

"What, you ran out of fingers and toes?"

"Polyphemus, really? Humor at a time like this?"

"Oh, don't go all Bogong on me." The stoic beast of darkness let a smile escape his grasp.

"You're having fun, all of you, look at yourselves; you're smiling, even gleeful!"

"Alright, Bogong. The tide is changing. Let them glimpse us but make them follow. Get clumsy with the sails, fain some distress." The bilges of The God of Peru began pumping. Bogong then removed his hand, and the ship would appear. He would lay his fingers down one after another against the mast, and parts of the ship would disappear and then reappear. "Tell the crew to spread their wings and reflect the rising sun straight into the Evil Eye."

"He will know our position." Morpho turned.

"He can't reach us with the harpoons from this distance. Though, he will certainly try." The harpoons, like mortars, streaked across the sky and fell just short of the hull. "The tide now, we take the tide and slip through the cave." The harpoons rained in with mighty splashes short of the hull. "That's it. Strong work. Lure those boats in. Send two Salvos into them, then drop the stern anchor." The shots released, and as if a mighty change in the direction of The God of Peru, the whole ship turned and headed for the Cave Sea. "Cut the anchor now!"

The Evil Eye could be seen burning orange and red. "There is a cloud of fire coming, Captain." Morpho turned and smiled.

"It's a swarm of Wasp. He's sending his foot soldiers."

"Who is he?" Francis whispered.

"He is the Second Orphan of Assisi. The Prince of Knowledge."

CHAPTER 38
"Silence"

The ship silently slipped through the rock. Francis marveled at the closeness of the stone and the azure blue water inside the cave.

"Captain, that swarm of Wasp. They will surely stand on the rim of the inner harbor and turn our trap against us."

"Have faith, Polyphemus. Remember, we called upon all allies."

The God of Peru emerged from the passage into the calm waters of the basin and the sheer cliff walls. "There, right there, put the port side against that wall and cloak us, Bogong!" The vine-like branches that intertwined the hull reached out and steadied the vessel against the rock face. Then, at once, they began to cover the ship in a shroud. Birds began to light upon the branches, and as Bogong wrapped his arms around the mast, the entire ship, with its protective canopy, disappeared from sight as if part of the cliff walls. "Silence."

The cliff walls began to hum with the sound of a thousand small wings. Francis looked towards the sky. Soldiers in black and auburn divisos, wearing helmets with reflective black eyes, paused on the cliff top and then plunged into the basin.

"Hold fast," the command came in a whisper. Francis stood and watched the legion scour the rock cliffs. Their swords, surging like stingers, plunged into the crevices of stone and branches.

"We know they're here," a voice rasped.

The first of three mercenary boats appeared, riding the waves in the mouth of the cave. The Wasp General flew and landed firmly on the deck of the vessel.

"Where are they?" He commanded.

"They're here," a mature voice stated calmly.

"They've vanished!" He roared. "They are not real."

"Do you see the anchor they left behind? It's real enough, and so are they. Circle the cliffs with your legion and wait for my command."

CHAPTER 39
"PURGE OUT THE FLIES"

"Captain, if we wait any longer to engage, we will not be able to sail back through the cave opening before it floods with water."

"Correct, we will not be leaving at least for another twelve hours."

"But won't we have to fight our way out at some point in time?"

"Do you remember Sun Tzu?" A smile crossed Adonis' face.

"Of course, he took Gastropoda with him and returned to help his people."

"Do you remember what he taught the armies of Gastropoda when they find themselves outnumbered?" Adonis looked into his memory.

"Yes, to put their backs against the mountain, and the enemies in a swamp and wait."

"The tide is not a problem. These pesky Wasp are not a problem. We have our backs against the mountain, and the Salt Lord is running out of time."

"Captain, he's moving boats forward. Orders, Sir?"

"Hold fast. Adonis, can you see the Salt Lord? Which vessel is he in?"

"He's at the back of the back cave. You see the boat with the net in the bow. Is he hiding a weapon?"

"There's a forward canon on the bow of every boat, but that's something he's saving for us."

"Your Orders Captain?"

"They can't see us. He's sending these few vessels forward to lure us into firing and revealing our position." The crew watched the Salt Lord's mercenaries course the azure waters of the cave lagoon. Francis watched the faces of his companions.

"You all are smiling like devils." Polyphemus raised his eyebrows at Bogong.

"The tide is rising, and they are terrified to be in here with us."

They fired their single cannons toward the cliff walls. Francis watched as the rock shattered and disappeared into the sea.

From the top of the cliffs, the Wasp General in his helmet of vietro commanded his lieutenants, "Purge out the flies!" The commandos leaped from the cliff walls in freefalls and hovered across the mirrored face of the ship.

"They can't see us?"

Adonis shook his head no. "They're trying to smell the sugar in our skin."

"He sends more boats." The vessels of the Salt Lord become confident in their own sight.

"They've gone. Never here. We're going to get trapped."

"What's your reckoning, Adonis? Is that all his vessels? How much more time do they have?"

"Maybe twenty minutes. I think he retains two vessels with him in the passage."

"Has he revealed his secret weapon?"

"No, it lies covered."

"Very good, prepare the guns."

Suddenly, the Wasp General is in front of the ship, smelling the sugar of their bodies. He raises his hand to signal to others, but another wasp's body plunges into him from the cliff edge. Both are squashed against the hull. Then, like rain from the heavens, the Wasp soldiers' bodies are flung out from the cliff and fall like hail, plunging into the vessels of the Mercenaries. Francis looked up the cliffs.

"It's the gold lions who play in the dunes at sunset! They're bantering the wasp. Look!" From the cliff face, there stepped a radiant black panther with gems about her neck and luring eyes. "It's the Princess of Cats! Felionia!"

Bogong, hugging the mast, turned his eyes upward. "I love kittens."

"She's looking right through me."

"She sees me too."

The Princess Cats drew an arrow across her bow, and it plunged through the branch covering and stuck in the ship's deck between Morpho's feet. All the crew looked forward. Morpho looked down... "Hmmm."

"I told you so, Morpho."
"Fire, the guns, Adonis!"
"Fire! Fire! Fire!"

Explosions of cannon fire ripped into the wooden vessels of the mercenaries. Francis watched as bodies, swords, and oars flipped through the sky. Cannon smoke filled the cave harbor, and the sound reverberated off the rock walls. His ears went silent with a shrill sound, and time slowed down as splinters of wood pierced the usable air.

The leaves of the tree branches coming from the Sacred shields began to turn fall colors and fall away. The tiny limbs and the mighty branches protecting the hull aged and recycled into the sea. The God of Peru floated loose from the rock wall. Francis looked up again and around the edge of the basin the paws and faces of giant cats could be seen resting in the sunlight.

"Captain! He's removed the net!" Morpho turned to face the cave and lunged towards the bow.

"Luna!"

CHAPTER 40
"The Salt Blade"

The Salt Lord's vessel rocked beneath the cave arch. A white-bladed sword was pressed to Luna's throat, and she screamed, "Father!" Draped in a black cape with salt stains, his voice moved his vessel forward. His mercenaries rowed the boat forward and guarded him with their bodies. "Seems we've found balance. You've taken much of mine, and now I've got a salt blade to your little heiress."

"Let her go!"

"One touch of this blade, and she turns to a pillar of Salt. Now, you listen. Call the kittens off and shackle your men to the deck. Hand and foot! Do it, or she dies!" He lifted Luna, his might deceiving.

Morpho turned and gazed up at the Princess of Cats. "Felionia, he has my daughter." He turned to the crew, and Adonis was binding his companions to the deck in irons. "No, Adonis, I can't ask this." Each looked up at him and tossed their weapons into a pile about the mast.

"You don't have too. Our bodies can be prisoners again, but our minds do not have to be." Adonis took his place among the others and shackled himself again.

"Just like old times!" Polyphemus turned and blew Felionia a kiss.

"You're all mad, like different human beings, relishing the chaos." Francis lifted his shackled wrist. "Won't he kill Morpho and then us?"

Adonis looked down the line. "Morpho is nearly immortal, protected by the Queen. He can only die by a needle dipped in spider venom and delivered through his body to wound the heart. The Queen makes this venom, but otherwise, the compounds are scarce and hard to find."

"So, they can stab him, crush him beneath this ship, and he will survive?"

"You've seen how maimed he can get. Look what he does to himself with nectar."

"Only his wife can kill him? And yet she sleeps with a different man every night? This is madness!"

Polyphemus leaned over and looked at Francis with seriousness. "The marriage bit, exactly, madness."

Bogong rustles his chains and speaks. "I marry my wives for one year with the option to renew."

"See there, that's brilliant!" Polyphemus was smiling.

Bogong nodded his mammoth head and displayed a toothy grin. "We write our names on a piece of paper. If we divorce, we rip the paper in two pieces. No woman has ever wished to divorce Bogong."

Polyphemus was nodding in agreement. "See, I can wrap my head around that! Maybe I should become an Ethiopian!"

As the Salt Lord's vessel touched the hull of The God of Peru, one, two, and then many of his mercenary guards leaped over the rail to the deck. White swords encircled Morpho. Their leader came to the royal Adonis. "Fancy colors are for girls. I'm going to take my time killing you all. Shark bait. I said, shark bait."

"Oh, how lovely." The mercenary's boot plunged into the chest of Adonis.

"You rather be salt, aye? I touch you like this, and you slowly turn to salt and drop off. You see yourself blow away in the breeze." Adonis remembered what that felt like while the leader waited for a response that never came.

The Salt Lord came over the rail with Luna in front of him and the blade to her neck. "Let her go, I will pay you in gold."

"Gold? Hahaha, do you think gold is enough? Have you not noticed all these beings around." He lifted his chin towards the cats, hissing down from the cliffs. "I said, call them off!"

"Why did you betray the kingdom and the Queen?"

"Betray? She gave me the backwater, the rejected tide." He spit on the deck of the ship." A new Kingdom is coming. One of Knowledge. You can't stop him. He sees and knows."

"I will give my life for hers!"

Luna shifted, "Father, no!"

"Luna, be still."

"Your life? What do I want with that, or this ship, or gold? The Prince of Knowledge is aligning the dark powers of the entire world. He sees I'm worth my salt. He promised me a kingdom."

"For what?"

"He wants the other Orphan." He motioned with his eyes to Francis.

"The Seventh Orphan, or she dies!" Morpho turned and looked at Francis.

"No, Father! Do not trade my life for Francis. I will live again in some way or form."

"No, No!"

Morpho charged the Salt Lord, and his mercenaries fell upon him with their swords. Bogong surged against the restraints, but Adonis's hand lifted. "Trust in him." Morpho stood with the white swords in his chest and blood filling his chest. The mercenaries expected him to turn ashen and fall, but Morpho's face turned otherworldly.

"I'm the King of Peru!" Morpho, taking both hands, grabbed the hilts of the swords in his chest and removed them in one swift motion, cutting mercenaries to their knees and driving their own blades into the back of their necks. In front of Francis's eyes, Morpho's chest wounds began to close. The blood stains on his vest began to disappear, and holes in the fabric mended themselves.

"No, no! One more move, and she dies. Remember Lot's wife? You saw what I did to her. I just whispered her name, and she looked back and became a pillar of salt! Is that what you want?"

"Fear not!" Francis had somehow torn through his iron shackles and stepped forward. Release her, and I will go with you." Morpho reached out his hand to hold Francis, but he was powerless to do so.

"Francis, this is impossible!" Francis turned and looked into Adonis's eyes.

"Control is not love."

"Well, right, the orphan has got some sense. Prepare the skiff; we're departing." Morpho stepped forward.

"You will never make it out of here alive. The water will crush your vessel against the top of the cave."

"Exactly. As I command, you will do or she dies!" He now held not just Luna but also Francis, who stood at his side. "You wanted to use your guns? Fire into the walls and open it up." Morpho was reluctant.

"You will still not make it out of here alive."

"Yeah, you're right. A little insurance policy." He drugged the white salt blade and grazed the skin of Luna.

"Ahh, it's burning!" Luna recoiled from the blade.

"She'll survive that with a little scar. The guns now, King!"

"Do not touch her again," Francis commanded.

"I'll do as I like, pup! The guns or she dies!"

Suddenly, Francis, with eyes interlocked with Luna's, stretched out his hand toward the cave, and a thunderbolt quenched the air. The cats above lept to safety, and the entire wall of stone exploded and teh debris settled into the dark sea.

"Well, now, we'll be leaving. Just one more quick thing." The Salt Lord drew the white blade entirely across Luna's shoulders and forearm.

CHAPTER 41
"Your Actions Are Misunderstood"

Luna collapsed into the arms of Morpho. Bogong snapped the chains that bound him and the others. "Dear God, she's collapsing from the pain." No one minded the Salt Lord or noticed the gaze of the Evil Eye was turned off.

"It's a flesh wound. It will take days to kill her." Morpho's eyes peered deep into Adonis's and could not respond. "Let's move her! Now! Now, to Diamond Back's surgery!"

"Has he any cure?" Morpho grasped Adonis' shoulder with the other hand over his mouth.

"He may, but we will need medicine from Gastropoda."

"Has he this medicine you speak of?"

"Morpho, brother. You are still weak, internally, from injuries, too. Doubtless, this is all, part of a larger plan laid out for our destruction. The Second Orphan remembered much about our lives. Are you with me? Can you focus, Morpho? Now then, let's move her to Diamond Back's surgery. I will stay with her, Morpho, and you can make a plan to rescue Francis."

Adonis stands before the physician. "Diamond Back, your actions are not understood."

"Well, you see, Great One, I'm just a simple sailor that tends to people. I'm not a healer, a doctor."

"I've seen you open a man's skull in Gastropoda and insert a piece of polished shell. I've seen you mix compounds to form cast and to set broken limbs. I've seen you diagnose everything from hernias to alopecia. You've worked alongside the doctors of Gastropoda and the Golden City, and now you say you're nothing but a simple sailor?"

"I have my own oaths to follow. She does not have value to this ship."

"Excuse me?"

"I tend those who give value to this ship."

"You discriminate in care? Our values do not align."

"Bogong, do you think Adonis is going to kill him?"

"I hope so. It's always the quiet ones who surprise you."

"He's a magnificent swordsman. Raised by the great Sulieman. Has he ever told you about carrying the sword of the prophet, David? You know, the one he used to cut off Goliath's head? Adonis has touched it and even wielded it. I saw it once in Constantinople. The sword of a shepherd, but alive. A simple black scabbard, large width blade, and a simple black handle wrapped in a thin silver inlaid cord. I vision David, just a shepherd boy raising it, putting a sandaled foot on the chest of the giant. Looking down the hole where the slung stone had pierced the head. Chopping, the head of Goliath off, then turning and lifting with both hands full of hair, for the Israelites to see. Can you imagine? Faithful Adonis, the most admired of all of us, cared for that sword in his youth..." Bogong turned to look at Polyphemus.

"I admire you."

CHAPTER 42
"Diamond Back"

"Captain."

"How is she, Adonis?"

"She's resting; Polyphemus and Bogong guard the door. Have you come up with a plan to save Francis?"

"Hmm?" Morpho returned to the chart desk.

"The Salt Lord has taken Francis to the deep-keeled vessel. The vessel shot a harpoon from offshore. The Salt Lord secured a line to the bow of his skiff, and it whisked them offshore. They're gone. Is it possible for us to follow his sea wake?"

"Possibly, but as the Salt Lord stated, the Second Orphan has been recruiting all manner to his cause. To engage hastily in open water would be a trap. Anyways, the only medicine that can save Luna is in Gastropoda."

"Will the Prince of Knowledge kill him?"

"No, he will first do to him as he did the First Orphan of Aissi."

"Adam?"

"Yes, the first man, and then he will do to him as he did the third Orphan."

"Jesus?"

"Yes, he will tempt him for forty days. So, our course of action must be to set sail for Gastropoda as quickly as possible. She will start to lose herself within days, and we will be stronger with the armada and Atlas on our sides. Excuse me, I must go to Luna, and we must prepare to sail."

"Captain, there's an issue. Diamond Back is discriminating care."

" Excuse me, he has taken the Hippocratic Oath. On what grounds is he not treating Luna?"

"He first said that he needed to mix compounds, then he needed some form of acupuncture. Ultimately, he is doing nothing because he does not see she has value to this ship. He is asking to see you." Morpho's face became red, and his eyes vacant. He turned and pulled a bow axe from the rail of the ship.

"Morpho, he's no good to anyone dead! These are perilous times!"

"Captain!"

"Out of my way!" The door to the surgery was locked, and Morpho kicked it open and hacked it off its hinges. Startled, Diamond Back fell from his chair to the deck boards and raised his bent arms like an earthly creature. Morpho, silent, pointed the axe toward him.

"Captain, I'm just a humble sailor. This; this delicate child, is beyond my skill, Sir. You see. I'm timid to touch her." Morpho stomped over the destroyed door, lifted Diamond Back with one hand, and lifted the blade of the bow axe to his neck. Diamond Back's eyes glazed over, and Morpho saw his cheeks elongate and his forehead sloped backward. The earthly creatures' arms were bending, and his color blended with the bulkheads. Morpho, seeing this transition, pulled him closer.

"What is this witchery? You're no Moth, you are a Praying Mantis!" The creature's eyes flashed, and the teeth of his forward jaw snapped over the axe's blade towards Morpho's face. Suddenly, Morpho felt a piercing pain run up his spine and pricked the antechamber of his heart. His eyes widened, and he stared into a face he hadn't seen in a long time.

"Moglie."

CHAPTER 43
"MOGLIE"

"Where is Moglie now?"

"Bogong has him in the brig; he cut off the weapon." Adonis entered the brig and stared at the person he had once known.

"New compounds, lost in the dunes? The wound of Luna, creating a slow death just so you could draw Morpho in. This is all too clever of a plan for you to develop independently." The creature's eyes reflected torch light. "We embraced you evidently, twice now, as a brother. Why Moglie?"

From a calloused throat came a demonic voice. "You could never understand that some of us were born evil. You and your Terms and Conditions of Freedom." He lunged and with crooked arms clasped the pinned flat bars of the cell. "Evil is Freedom! Evil is power! To slave an innocent and to beat it and to feed itself it's own dung is the greatest feeling in life!"

Adonis turned. "Lock the door."

Morpho lay on a table beside his daughter. The evidence of poison formed at the corners of his mouth. Adonis touched him, connected in his dream state. Then a mighty thundering could be heard as if the cliffs walls may tumble in upon them.

All hands ran to the forward deck and looked toward the night sky. Red lights illuminated the shadowy shape of a Black Widow traversing the sky. "It's the Queen's constellation. It tracks her movements as her army moves at night."

"And the thundering?"

"She's riding Pegasus!"

CHAPTER 44
"MY QUEEN"

The Queen dropped from the cliffs on a delicate silk cord. Her artisan made armor was black and form-fitting. Her swords drew straight lines down her thighs, a belt of intertwined rings about her waist. She moved erratically about the deck, retreating and advancing from the pools of blood that she knew seeped from her beloved. "Take me to them."

She entered the surgery one foot in front of another, fell upon her beloveds and kissed each one again and again.

Later, she came to sit in front of Adonis. "We saw the blue glow of the Sacred Ornaments. They produce their own star sign in the heavens so allies will know where they are needed. We were nearing the Golden Kingdom and came upon Pegasus, but Pegasus, too, had seen the star sign. He prayed to his ancestors, and they came. He was not alone but one of many. I connected through the dream state, not only to Pegasus, but Morpho. I tried Luna, but she was blocked by something."

"The Salt Lord kept her veiled with a net. None of us could reach her."

"But I am her mother. I should never be out of touch with my daughter." She looked accusingly into Adonis' blue eyes and found her own guilt. "The Seventh Orphan has been taken?"

"He traded his life for Luna's. He was under much distress to save her as much as Morpho. So much that his powers made manifest." Her brown eyes widened. "He tore metal as parchment, and with one impulse of his hand, he brought down the entire mountain. The Second Orphan has him. Morpho's plan was to take Luna to Gastropoda for healing. From there, we would resupply and find him. Do you have an antidote for the venom delivered to the antechamber of Morpho's heart?"

"I do, but if they've plotted a deception so well for us, they've certainly factored in the possibility that we may reach him in time."

"You mean they've enhanced the venom to something they only have the treatment for?" She nodded her head and then began to cry.

Before There Were Flowers

"I cannot lose them."

"My Queen." She reached for Adonis' hands.

"Please call me Theridiidae in our privacy. I need that comfort."

"Theridiidae, we can set sail with Morpho and Luna. Our sea path to Gastropoda is clear. We will follow the star until Atlas sees us and the armada meets us, but this will take days. And in days, Luna will begin to lose herself, and Morpho will deteriorate significantly. I will return them both to you."

"Her eyes leaped up. I'm not leaving them." He stood with her and reached for her hand, but she turned away.

"I know this is hard. Torn between service to Kingdom and family. If we do not set sail with haste, they both will die. If you leave the Gold Coast now, the entire Kingdom may fall." She walked and stood between Morpho and Luna.

"Even if you all were to spread your wings, would there be enough canvas on The God of Peru to speed yourselves in time to Gastropoda?"

The sound of a cat landing on its paws came from the deck above. They both registered the slight sound that Morpho said something.

"Sailish." They looked back, and the captain's jacket was turning hard at the tips of the shoulders. Adonis laid his hand in Morpho's, and Theridiidae's ear went to his mouth. "Pegasusish prays to the east."

"What did he say?"

"That our hopes lie in Pegasus. He says Pegasus prays to the east. How many of Pegasus' family came with him?"

"An entire herd."

Adonis looked into her eyes. "That's a mighty canvas!"

CHAPTER 45
"The Queen of the New Moon"

Arriving on deck, torches of oil cloth burned as Adonis gave orders. "Prepare the ship for Gastropoda."

"What of Moglie?"

"He stays with the ship Bogong. He may be a source of information along the way."

Sitting on a cask was a woman adorned in furs about her shoulders and waist. A helmet of thin matted metal with bronze eyes was upon her head. She lifted her face plate to reveal a visage more delicate than the mask. "Felionia." She bounced to Adonis and swirled into his embrace. "You came in our hour of need." She nuzzled his hand as he embraced her face.

"Adonis?" Adonis turned, and behind him was the Queen. He stepped aside, and the Princess of Cats bowed and stretched her hands before her.

"My Queen." The Spider Queen stepped forward. Kneeling, she grasped the soft furs on Felionia's shoulders and lifted her chin.

"Rise, Felionia." The Queen held the paw-gloved hands. "I know you loved Morpho when he was a soldier."

"I loved him as a man."

"I always assumed you hated me for stealing his love away."

"You didn't give him a choice. It was love you or die, it still is." The Queen turned away.

"You speak boldly to me. Obviously, you still love him."

"I saw the glow in the sky from the Sacred Ornaments. I knew not what countrymen were in need but that my countrymen needed me." She walked to the rail beside the Queen.

"Theridiidae, I did not lose my lover, I lost my turn. He became a soldier; he became a prisoner of war. Then he became an entirely different being."

"Did me stealing him cause your life to change into the role you play today?"

"I wanted to be a mother, yes, and the void left by him could only be filled by the distraction and manipulation of many men."

"Do you have children now?"

"Yes, I have lovely children. Children who would never be if I were the wife of the faithful Morpho."

"So, he has never returned to you?"

"Never, not even in his mind, and I think that is why I can say I love him better now than I ever did back then."

"Admiration?"

"If so, it's now respect. He loves you. Therefore, I love you. You together love your daughter; therefore, I love her as if she were my daughter. You both give your lives to serve not only this country but the world. Therefore, I love this country and the world."

"That's how his love made you change?"

"Losing his love could only have been replaced by something as large as the world."

Queen looks over the water. "I feel I'm a failure. This strategy was never supposed to become part of me." She looked over for answers. "How do you do it?"

"A woman can take many strangers to bed and still be a wonderful mother, a faithful wife, and an incredible leader of her people."

"How? I'm a Queen asking for council."

"Every heart resonates with truth. Before you can ever be honest with others, you must be honest with yourself. Theridiidae, do not listen to others, and do not listen to what your mind tells you about yourself. Consume only truth, speak only truth, and every heart will resonate with your words."

"Felionia, I must go with my family to Gastropoda. I can only leave the Kingdom in the care of someone who loves me, and this country will only follow the leadership of a strong woman." Her hands slid down the shapely arms. "Obviously, you know how to command men. Will you be my General and rule in my stead?" Felionia bowed her head. The Queen kissed each shoulder of Felionia, and then her head between the cat-like ears of her helmet, and the bronze details in the matted black metal was now accented with a crimson line of spider red.

Adonis and Polyphemus assembled the Sacred Ornaments in a circle on the forward deck. The crew placed the beds of Morpho and Luna in the center. All formed around them within the Sacred Ornaments. The Queen stepped between the beds and placed a shell upon each shield. "Never in this Kingdom has there been such an assembly. Tonight, we gather ourselves together to collect courage, faith for healing, and safe passage for all travelers between life and death." All the warriors drew their swords and turned the blades upward, behind their backs, and crossed the hilt of each sword. Pegasus with his holy ancestors each kneeling surrounding the warriors and stretched their wings forming a nest reflecting the blue glow of the Sacred shells. "Stand I, stand we, stand all who have faith in truth. Before there were flowers, there was faith, hope, and love." The shells began to glow on each breast, and the gold calligraphy of every name set free began to be written upon the shells, the shields, across the deck, up the legs and wings and swords of all assembled. Spheres of blue and gold arced over the raised sword tips of every warrior, as the oil cloth torches went out. Trace elements of color coursed in the dome, and a new color was formed. Morpho's hard edges disappeared, the new color filled his being, as his eyes awoke. His torso raised, and he lifted his arms, and light balanced upon him. The cape around Luna formed from beneath her, and salt wounds that once had been burns turned to words of fine-lined calligraphy tattooed upon her skin. The cape was illuminated in shades of pale green, gold, and brown hues. Her body lifted upright in the light, and the Queen of New Moon was born.

CHAPTER 46
"The Queen Removes Her Armor"

"Morpho, are you awake?" The King's eyes opened.

"Theridiidae. Is Luna safe?"

"She's fallen back to sleep." He turned his head to see her. "You must lay still. The needle Moglie used is still lodged in the antechamber of your heart. The surgeons of Gastropoda will remove it before it disintegrates. We set course for the star of Gastropoda momentarily." He looked into her eyes.

"You are coming with us?" She nodded.

"The Kingdom?" She laid her fingers across his lips and stroked the winged cape from his shoulders.

"The Kingdom will be protected by Felionia in my absence. She will be my sister, General, from now on. She left this talisman of her love for you." She placed a golden pendant in his hand and closed the fingers.

"You are wise; she is pure of heart and faithful." He looked longingly into the Queen's eyes, her helmet at his feet, her arm so finely fitted to her form, and the red swords upon each thigh.

"Theridiidae?"

"Shh, save your breath. We prepare to sail and must move you below deck."

The God of Peru plunged into the Gold Coast Sea, and as all sails were set, Pegasus moved to the ship's bow. His ancestors stood in the formation of a spear behind him, and they knelt with their own Sacred breastplates around each neck. The herd spread their mighty wings as sails; their dream state became the ship's dream state and sped across the sea toward the star of Gastropoda.

"Adonis, who mans the helm?"

"No man, the Sacred Ornaments are fixed on the star. It's just like the ancient Greeks. Their ships had no rudders but were directed by the will of their hearts. At this speed, we will meet Atlas's eyes at dawn. Possibly, the Armada if he saw the glow of the Sacred Ornaments as did our other allies."

"Blessed assurance."

"Yes, I suggest we all rest. Pegasus stands watch."

The Queen removed her armor. "Theridiidae, will you lay upon me?" She moved to Morpho and laid her hand on his chest.

"I might kill you."

Morpho looked at her and smiled. "You haven't yet, why not?"

The Queen's eyes responded, and she looked innocent, like a young girl. "You were the first one to fight for me." She took his hand and set with her head close to his. "I would go at sunset and walk down those dusty corridors of prisoners. Watching fear fill their faces, knowing that tonight may be the last night of their lives. I selected one, one who had become their leader, feared by all. I turned to walk away, and I heard your voice challenge him, a fight to the death just to have one night with me. Knowing that I would kill you in the morning. Never had someone ever fought for my love. I thought he would surely kill you, but you still had my respect. They released you, and in the setting sun, you stepped from the cave cell and dusted off your uniform. I will never forget that moment. The jacket and the white pants were stuffed inside the black boots. They drew out a circle and laid quartz stones around it. They lit torches that burned the same color as the setting sun. They offered you each a sword and you tossed yours to your enemy, and you said, *'I will make her my own,'* and no one laughed. I've never seen a bull dispatched so cleanly, professionally, and with his own sword. You were taken and washed and washed again, your uniform laundered and pressed, your skin rubbed with oil, and your hair perfumed. I was giddy as a girl in dance. They opened the terraced doors, and you were brought by candle into the night. No fear in your eyes. You kissed each of my cheeks and then my forehead. You poured my wine, broke my bread, and dismissed my servants, saying you would feed me. You talked of ideas, concepts, and plans for the future. When you kissed my lips, you said, *'this is the only moment of the rest of my life. I will spend it loving you without any reservation.'* You moved me and the chair. Lifted me, but not to the normal bed. You went inside and suddenly cast pillows and carpets and drapery outside. You made this bohemian pallet beneath the stars. You extinguished the candles save two. You made me to lie down and you loosened your clothes. You fed me figs, and cheese, and chocolate and sipped the wine but made me taste it from your lips. You made me warm and full, and when the night breeze blew, you built a fire from the furniture. You turned me over and made me call you my King, and when I did, you pledged your allegiance and made me your Queen. When the sun was about to rise, you had me again. Then you took juice from the fig, and you wrote both of our names on a piece of paper, and you folded it and placed it in this very locket around my neck. You said, *'I will never seek to control you. Your body and who you give it to is entirely up to you. I will love you for being exactly who you are, even if it kills me. Therefore, what love you choose to give me is a pure, unrepayable gift of mutual respect that I can trust.'* The dawn came because time waits for no one, even love, and another life was taken in your stead, and Nine months later, Luna was born. Most men waste the last night of their lives begging, weeping, and confessing to Gods they've never served. Yet you lived that night remarkably and created the most enchanting evening of my life."

Morpho listened and then said. "Every sailor lives assuming that each sunset will be their last."

Tears were dripping down Theridiidae's face, and she whispered. "You've given me so much Freedom, support, and unconditional love. What have I given to you?"

With one hand Morpho reached up and covered hers and the other he stretched out and took the hand of Luna and then spoke. "You gave me my life."

CHAPTER 47
"A CATALYST"

"Father."

"Luna, you are awake. You're just lying there?"

"I have not been able to sleep. Every time I fall, I jolt myself awake. I have no control over it. It is as if my body is too weary to rest." Morpho made to lift himself.

"Father, may we have an intellectual conversation?"

"Like when you were a child over a dinner?"

"Yes, we would sit to eat, and you'd say, *'let's have an intellectual conversation. Ask me anything, and I will tell you everything I know about it.'* It made me think about ideas; I didn't just see myself; I learned to see myself as part of the entire world. Father, I've always heard the legend of your immortality; I think that's why I've never really worried when you have been gone. I just always knew in my mind that you would return, but when I saw those men stab you with their swords, the blades punctured your chest so effortlessly. I was overcome with the realization that you could be gone. Then, as if in a dream, you did not fall, you did not wither, you grabbed them about their necks, and you yelled like some ancient god into their faces. You grasped their swords that were lodged in your chest, pulled them out, and slaughtered them as swine. I can't get that image out of my mind. I cannot comprehend life without you. And yet here we both are, frail as dried flowers, you with a venomous needle in the antechamber of your heart. How am I supposed to survive in a world where I've lost the very creators of my life? I don't have any adult answers."

There was the silence of an intelligent listener.

"Luna, a person never outgrows their need for a father or a mother. There are times in everyone's life when they feel alone and without any adult answers. There was a time before there were flowers when butterflies clung to the bark of trees for sustenance and companionship. I've often wondered how desperate life must have been for them. Being in the world and feeling you belonged in the world, yet there seemed to be no meaning in your existence. I've always thought that the beauty of

Before There Were Flowers

a butterfly's wings reflected their partner, the flower, but then I realized that they had this beauty even before the catalyst to their lives was born. What is impressive is that they did not perish. They prepared a garden, and one day, their flowers of purpose bloomed."

"A catalyst?"

"Yes, a catalyst is a person who will propel your life forward, giving it more meaning than you could have ever done alone. Sadly, one day, time will not allow your mother and I to walk this mortal path with you. One day, we will only see and talk to each other in the dream state, but there will be a new person or people who will not fill the exact role, but will play an equal and possibly a more powerful role in your life as time passes."

"Father, when the Salt Lord had the blade to my throat and he wanted Francis, there was something inside of me that was not scared but wanted to protect him. Then, when Francis tore through the iron and bartered his life for mine, there was something inside of me that screamed out in defiance. I know it was not from these wounds." She touched the scars that had transformed on the tapestry of her skin. "When he lifted his hand, that was the reason I fainted."

"What do you mean?"

"I mean that all the energy that passed through his body to bring down the mountain felt like it came from my soul. Now that he has been taken, I can't reach him in my dream state. Does that mean he is..."

"No, no, not at all. Though he is young, Francis may have more strength than all of us. He was born alone, has lived alone, and is now becoming a man."

"Yes, but Father, he now is face to face with the Devil."

"Luna, I'd say he's seen that face almost every night of his life and has not perished."

"The power that came through his hand. Enough power to turn rock into dust. Have you seen that before?"

"No, I think in that moment Francis' catalyst was realized."

"How does that happen?"

"A moment of collision of fundamental things."

"What are these fundamental things?"

"Faith, hope, and love."

CHAPTER 48
"THE A RELATIONSHIP"

The Queen stands behind the helm of The God of Peru and watches it steer itself. "Do you know this ship well, Senora?"

"Polyphemus, Good morning." The Queen wrapped her arms around the disgraced Centurion for comfort. His scarlet cape matched the thin red tattoos laid on her skin. "Sadly, no. To be honest, Morpho speaks of her as another lover, which makes me incredibly jealous." She turned and placed her hands against the wood flesh of another mistress. "But now I see her differently." Polyphemus stepped beside her as the Sun rose. "You know the world is controlled by Women. The Moon, the Sea, our Mother Earth. Males are here to serve. Just look at the Sun; so many worship him, but he is just chasing her, hoping for another glance at the Moon."

"I've always loved the night and its activities."

"That's because you are a Moth."

"Hmm, I've never thought of it that way. If you're jealous of this ship and it taking Morpho away, do you think that is why your protection of him gets weaker the further he gets away? You know, the changing of his visage into a different form."

"I've never seen him in that way. I've always seen him as the regal King."

"Oh wow, that's fantastic."

"But yes, I've been foolish like a first wife; that will never happen again. I'm horrified that I ever took him for granted and sought to change him. I could have easily changed him into someone who no longer wanted me. This ship, this ship, has carried more of his burdens than I, his wife. I blocked so much of him, so much more I could have had if I hadn't assumed he would always just be there. Morpho has been my sun. Even when I've hidden my face from him, he's never failed to search for me. That was not a weakness in him-to love me unconditionally. The universe gave me a leader of love, and I stamped him inappropriately as my soulmate. I do not own him, and every moment he chooses to give me is the perfect gift that I can enjoy right now."

"This vessel upon the sea gives us forgiveness."

"Forgiveness for what, Polyphemus?"

"Hmm, we've each played different roles in life. None of us ever refer to ourselves as good. Now, we do good things for good people, and we do very bad things to bad people. The ship is like a mother. She loves us no matter what we do."

"Is that why you've always been a bachelor?"

"Hmm, no. I've always wanted a relationship that resembled the capital form of the letter A. Two individuals who lean entirely on each other with like minds and connecting hearts. That triangle shape is the strongest structural shape in the world. If something falls mightily upon it, then the something breaks, not the relationship. Most people have a relationship that resembles the letter H. Two individuals in an agreement of life partnership. If anything falls upon that, it immediately separates them and brings destruction."

"That's a beautiful way of describing it. Did you come up with that?"

"Oh no, that was Adonis, of course, but it always stuck with me."

"But he hasn't been married in centuries."

"You are right, but he still walks with her in Gastropoda. Not even death could destroy their relationship."

Bogong snapped his fingers, and the Queen and Polyphemus turned to face the sun.

"They've sighted whales off the starboard bow. It's the armada of Gastropoda."

CHAPTER 49
"Self Care"

"Where is Gastropoda?"

"There, my Queen, do you see the bank of clouds? Alright, hold your gaze there. You will glimpse it and then eventually realize it." She held her gaze and then realized that the peaks of Gastropda were snow-capped, and what she had mistaken for clouds was the steam of the volcanos.

There were no soundings from the sculptural shells along Lungomare save one low burst. The dolphins and whales did not play but were as vigilant as eagles. "Have you ever been to Gastropoda before?"

"Yes, Morpho and I spent the first years of our marriage here. We lived in the Villa of Endless Moons, and Luna was born there."

"Did you sail here aboard The God of Peru?"

"No, that was before. We sailed in a vessel Morpho had bartered for in Venice. Deep-keeled, a salon, and letto. He would tie the rudder fast, and we would fall into a hammock at sunset in a tangle of arms and legs. When it stormed, he would wrap and tether the extra sails and oars and toss them overboard as a sea anchor, keeping the bow into the waves. We were at the mercy of the sea, and yet I felt the most safe I ever have in his arms. Life upon that vessel was so simple. There were no titles, no kingdoms, no armies nor invaders. Just us and the promise of our future."

The ancient King Bianchi stood with his son King Garbo and Atlas on the top of the high mountain. "Unto Death." The promise echoed amongst the jungle along Lungomare. Launches created from giant mussel shells rowed out into the harbor, cast lines to the bow of The God of Peru, and towed the vessel to a stone pier. The armies of Gastropoda lined the stone pier with banners unfurled. Morpho and Luna were taken on litters, each led by a Warrior. Adonis accompanied Theridiidae, following behind. When they turned to walk between the armies, an order was given, and golden swords with pearl handles were raised in a protective arc.

"Queen Theridiidae, Welcome home." The Queen walked and embraced Garbo. As she did, she reached out to the kneeling Atlas, lifted his tear-covered face, and kissed it.

"This is not your fault. Now, join your King and brothers." With her arms around Garbo's shell, she disappeared to the Villa of Awareness.

"Theridiidae, your villa is waiting for you. I know that time is of the essence, but you've done all you can right now and made good choices. You must accept self-care. Without self-care, you will not be able to care for others. I know this is difficult, but it is imperative. When you have centered, we will plan together to meet everyone's needs. Will you trust me? Tune your mind to silence and repair your body in the dream state."

CHAPTER 50
"A HISTORY"

Morpho was placed upright in the same surgeon shell he had inhabited before. The clear gel incased his body and held him upright. Luna lay inside in a clamshell bed attended by nurses and doctors in the villa but in a cognizant state.

"Do these scars burn?"

"No, Mother, at least not when you touch them." Theridiidae ran her finger over the gold tattoos, and each glistened in the morning light. "What are they? I mean, what do they say?" The Queen pronounced each word. "Is that an ancient tongue?"

"A very ancient tongue."

"What do they say?"

"It's a code of validation. It's hard to explain. It's as if each phrase is a symbol of the stars at significant events in human history. It's a record of astronomical events."

"A history?"

"Yes, seven points in history."

"And I am to be a part of them or a Sayer of these events?" Luna pulled at the skin and tried to decipher them. "I did not choose these things, these markings or star signs. Mother, who chose them? Who wrote this story on my life?"

"I don't have the answers Luna, but we will talk to Garbo and Adonis." The Queen lifted the wing of Luna. "These are just tiles in the wing. The weavers of Gastropoda are very good. They can mend this." Luna pulled the wing back and rolled over to face the window. "Luna."

"Excuse me. The Council is assembled; we are in the garden." The Queen watched Adonis walk away, his blue cape of wings lifting in the breeze. She turned to Luna and kissed her wet cheek.

"Let's hold hands and communicate in the dream state." Garbo leads the Council, standing in his garden. "The power of the Priest is growing. He is collecting orphans, even stealing children from islands all over the

Caribbean. Having lost Francis, the Seventh Orphan, he is in debt to the Evil Eye. The Eye cannot exist if people do not believe in it. So, it is hungry for orphans and slaves; those it can feed its lies or beat into them. The slave markets of Labadee are growing, and the smoke rising from the sugar plantations of Bermuda turns the sky black. The Evil Eye feeds its lies like sugar to the enslaved. It is a drug. Once consumed, the body feels it cannot exist without it. Atlas, please tell us what you've seen with your eyes." Atlas, stepped forward in blaze and bronze colors having matured.

"When I look back, I see a dark sky, dark enough that it has shaded the sun. The sea is no longer blue and flows not to this place, but from it. Ships course there. One is larger than all the others, but nonetheless has the same design with black sails. They seem to be on the same heading, not for war or for conflict, but for conquering. The larger vessel has a mighty power within it. A strong Eye can be seen hovering above it. It draws all manner of ancient sea creatures to it. I observed one instance above the sunken Bahamian island, the City of Great Wealth. This person dressed in a vestiture of black was rowed by slaves above the sunken city, and from the depths came tentacles. Tentacles so large they could've crushed the vessel unexpectedly, but instead, it delivered three stone sarcophagi with these symbols." He knelt, scattered sabbia across the white garden stones, and drew the symbols. Adonis moved forward in the blink of an eye and swept them away.

"Thank you, Adonis." Garbo lifted his eyes and quoted quickly. "Upon this solid rock, I stand."

The Council retorted. "All others are sinking sand!"

"Is this the Priest? This being in black that barters with the ancient sea beast?" Atlas stepped back, and Garbo commenced.

"No, he is the Second Orphan, the oldest living human being in the world today. He is called The Prince of Knowledge and has been very patient and cunning."

"You knew him?"

"I knew him as a boy."

"Atlas, did you see anything else yesterday? Anything of Francis?" Atlas shook his head.

"I know Francis is aboard the largest vessel, the same vessel the sarcophagi were transported. At last light I saw what appeared to be smaller portions of the dark cloud break off and move out to sea but they dropped away like fog upon the water. Maybe they were just clouds or flying fish."

Adonis stepped forward in interest. "Could he really be using fish, and if he could be using fish, then wouldn't he control the entire sea?"

"I've only heard the Prince of Knowledge referred to as Prince of the Air. I've only known of one Orphan to walk on water."

"And their sarcophagus?"

"It was stolen from his tomb on the third day." Everyone turned and looked at Polyphemus.

CHAPTER 51
"A Water Better Than Nectar"

Torches illuminate the surgeon's shell where Morpho abides. "Bogong?"

"I am here." The jungle foliage manifested into a man.

"We've come to sit with him and visit you too." Theridiidae leaned up and kissed the dark, chiseled cheek of the protector.

"Here is a basket of food. Stand down. Polyphemus, Atlas, Adonis, Garbo, we are all here."

"I forget the water here is better than nectar." Polyphemus lifted a cup to Atlas.

"From the snow of the High Mountain, it flows from the waterfalls into the lava and filters. This whole island is like an eternal spring." Atlas poured water for Adonis.

"Do you remember Cana, when Jesus attended that wedding with his mother, and they ran out of wine?"

"You mean when his mother asked him, isn't there something you can do?"

"He asked the boys to fill the urns with spring water, and they drank it and thought it the finest of wine." Bogong, who had said nothing, suddenly leaned forward.

"My wives are not nectar or wine but pure water from deep wells." Theridiidae touched his shoulders.

"You're missing them; you cannot live without them?"

"It is the first time that I've ever had this feeling. A mournful feeling. I'm not worried for them, and I'm not worried for myself. It's just this sudden burden that has been wrapped around me that my time with them is so incredibly precious."

The Queen looked to Garbo and Adonis. "I have several questions. What does Atlas's vision mean? The retrieval of these sarcophagi and the symbols you erased so quickly in the sand. And above all, how do we reach Francis?"

"They are trying to synthesize his catalyst by raising the tombs of former orphans."

"The tombs of Adam and Christ?"

"His catalyst? I don't understand."

"Theridiidae, every orphan that has been born has had a catalyst, another person who propels them to realize their powers or life's work."

"Does this person have powers?"

"I guess that could be argued. So far, history has only recorded male orphans, and therefore, we can only trace their catalysts, which have always been manifested by love."

"But you speak of Adam and Christ, and I know now of this Prince of Knowledge, and there is Francis, but not all of these were orphans."

"Yes, but all were abandoned by their parents at some point and time."

"So, these beings were born and then suffer severe emotional abandonment by their parents. Am I right?"

"You are. Christ wept drops of blood over the abandonment of his Father."

"Well, they survived then."

"I'd say that they dealt with it, consumed it, and turned that pain into their power, maybe unknowingly."

"And then what?"

"Then, as you say, this other person comes along, and they fall in love. Let me see, Adam loved Eve enough to abandon the garden built by his father. Christ loved Mary so much that he could raise the dead. Now Francis destroying the rock." The Queen stood abruptly.

"Oh God, oh God, the clouds that broke away at sunset! We are being attacked! We are being attacked! They want Luna!"

CHAPTER 52
"Unto Death"

Bogong dropped his lunch, drew his swords, and stood guard before his Master. The Sacred Ornaments had been stored away. The others fled to the Villa of Endless Moons, and as they did, it seemed like asteroids of fire began to fall. The clouds of Gastropoda turned black with swarms of Wasp. Theridiidae leaped the walls of the Villa, drew her red swords, and dipped them in venom. She dove through the balcony door of Luna's room as four wasps entered. She rolled and cut them down in one swoop of her movements. "On your feet, child!" She tossed Luna one of her swords, and she caught it in mid-air. "We are moving to Pinnacles." Coursing the halls of the Villa, they touched palms once and connected in the dream state. "Let's slow it all down." As they ran, time turned slowly. The flight and spiral of arrows could be followed with their eyes. Their moments were fast and intertwined, rolling, spinning, cutting down each other's foes. They escaped the house to the jungle outcropping of obelisks."

"Mother, stop. Why are we fleeing? Shouldn't we be going to protect Father?" Theridiidae turned with fear in her eyes. "What weapons did you claim from the Wasp, child?"

"Here, take back your sword. I gathered plenty, Mother." Luna wrapped a scarf around her waist, and there harbored two short swords. She leaned and took up a bow and quiver of arrows and missed her mother's voice.

"You didn't answer me. Can you hear me, Luna? Your tattoos are glowing and changing."

"What! What does that mean?"

"Someone is, is seeking you."

"Seeking me! Seeking me for good or for evil?"

"Listen, I knew not before what I know now. They are not attacking Gastropoda. Their reason for being here is to take you."

"To take me? Why? What do I have to do with this? Because I'm your daughter?"

Theridiidae stopped the ascent and turned back again. "Down!" Two stinger arrows flew at Luna's wings. "Because Francis is in love with you. You are his catalyst. No, get on your feet!" The two shot up the steep hill.

"He loves me!" Theridiidae glanced back and saw happiness on Luna's face.

"Return fire and stop showing your teeth with that smile. It's a great target for them."

"Mom, Mom, let's show them how to fight like girls!"

The Wasp swarmed the beach, the villages, the hillsides, and the port of Lungomare. They came to the surgeon's giant shells and flipped, turned, and swarmed again and again, taking in the image of Morpho upright in the cocoon. "This is the captain. Where's the girl?"

"He's dead already."

"Not dead enough. Someone's got to pay for the General."

The group rose in the air, and their stinger blades glistened. They dove in quick succession, and as if there was a Sacred invisible shield over the giant Shell, they were cut down. "What? What?" Others dove and stopped short, peering into a mirror that reflected themselves. One reached a hand forward, and the mirror rippled.

"It's a trick!" His head was removed by something invisible to all. Another group came seeing the bodies of nest members. They dove toward the shells and surrounded it with stinger blades drawn.

"Wait," the leader stood cautiously. "It's the Captain of that ship. They left him unguarded." The leader stopped the Wasp from moving forward with his sword. Never taking his eyes off the shell, he knelt down and used the tip of his sword to flick Wasp's blood onto the mirror. His reflective eyes revealed a huge figure. Bogong, never revealing himself, cut the hoard down. More came but did not engage. They called to others, and they came. In front of the shell stood a blood-splattered image of a man-shaped Sacred ornament.

"It's a warrior."

"Just one of them?"

"There's heaps of dead." The dead corpses of Wasp began to be piled in defensive places in front of the shell, and then from within the blood-splattered image, a glowing blue could be seen raised, and from it came a sound.

The wasp dove in swarms. Like a whirlwind, the cloak of wings turned to blood. The wasps were repelled as if swatted down by a mighty hand, but the fury of the swarm attracted more until the air around Morpho was a deafening roar of wings.

The armies of Gastropoda stood from the High Mountain and fired arrows at will into the swarms. Every arrow found a mark, and yet the swarms persisted. "Was that shell horn of Bogong?" Like the mechanical components of a clock, the three brothers in arms worked together, clearing the Wasp.

"He's in need. They are in danger!" They moved-jumping, flying, wielding their weapons like conductors. Over rocks and through the jungle, the arrows whizzed above, Wasp fell, and yet they came sucking the air for sugar.

When they reached the glen of the surgeon's shell, no more Wasp were present. Clearing the area with swords and bows drawn, they stepped over hundreds of dead. "Bogong, Bogong, Bogong!" They yelled, calling out in desperation, but the quiet voice, 'I am here' did not come." They moved to the shell of Morpho, and a tapestry of dripping blood covered the tomb.

"Are these swords?"

"Stingers, oh God."

Adonis and Polyphemus touched the giant shoulders of Bogong, and his body was revealed.

"He covered Morpho with his body. His wings a shield." They pulled each blade that pinned his corpse to Morpho's. When they removed the body of Bogong his arms had been surrounding Morpho to shield his King.

"It's both of them. Both of them are gone."

Adonis stepped forward and wrapped the cape of Bogong around them both in a tight embrace. We move to the Pinnacles with Theridiidae. As they ran to reach them, the Armies of Gastropoda directed their fire at the mass swarm around the monolithic stones of the pinnacles. The ancient King Bianchi had moved slowly and carefully to the mountain edge. His eyes were wide apart, taken in by the attack on his peaceful Kingdom. Those who had recited the Terms and Conditions of Freedom fought for it and won the villages, the beach, and the strada of Lungomare. He had seen the swarm form around Bogong and Morpho. He had seen the smile on Luna's face and the aura of her and her mother in unison. "Unto

Death," he commanded, protecting fire to be sent around them.

"Are you ready, Luna?" The Queen and Luna stood in the middle of the great stones back-to-back.

"Is there a plan?"

The Queen nodded her head with her eyes vigilant on the jungle. "Yes, these are not our enemies. These are beings we just want to kill."

Luna's head turned back. "Are you giving me Freedom? Freedom to enjoy this?"

"Freedom is our catalyst to love."

"I'm fighting for Francis, for you, Father, Gastropoda, and all that I love."

They spun, dove wielding their weapons, driving back the hoards. The other warriors joined them. "What is that? Coming from the jungle. Did you glimpse it?" Atlas and Adonis turned quickly and clashed swords. "Iguanas." The arrows of Gastropoda bounced from the armor of the iguanas. Their eyelids rolling back and protecting them. Slowly, the circle of warriors was falling back to the protection of each other in the center of the Pinnacles.

"Form a shield wall around Luna," the Queen commanded. Seeing they had them, the Wasp stopped, and the iguanas crawled forward, licking their bone-teethed lips.

"We will not give up." The warriors were itching for more. Polyphemus retrieved his sword from the body of a wasp, wiped the blade, and yelled a battle cry into the encroaching foe. Fear caused the Wasp to tremble.

"Come on, come on." An iguana lunged forward, and Atlas ran his blade through the soft spot of armor. Then, the thunder of avalanche could be heard from the High Mountain. Adonis lifted his eyes and saw a large swath of jungle being pushed aside as if elephants were charging.

"Unto Death, unto Death!" The piercing battle cry of the Ancient Bianchi was echoing off the cliff walls of the Island, and all inhabitants turned to witness a giant snail tumbling and rolling for the swarm in the pinnacles.

"Move!" Adonis shouted, and the group fell back and dove outside the pinnacles. The Ancient King's shell collided with monolithic stones and shattered into waves of millions of tiny sharp fragments. The host of enemies hit by the blast were destroyed.

CHAPTER 53
"WHAT are YOU Saying"

The group of warriors began to stand up and help each other. The great vertical stones were shattered. The Queen, having looked Luna over for injuries, surveyed the debris. "Bianchi, I have never seen such a selfless act from a King." She moved slowly, and her gaze fell upon the men. "What? What are you saying?" Adonis' lips had never moved. She looked to Polyphemus and then to Atlas. "What are you saying!" Then she turned toward the valley and yelled. "Bogong! Bogong! Bogong!" But the ever-enduring reply never came. She began to run. Her helmet and coat of arms about her, the red swords in each hand. She continually yelled out his name because where he was, so was her husband.

When Theridiidae entered the glade, she stopped short. The bodies of Wasp lay piled, and as she walked to the surgeon's shell, she could see the gel was pulled out and no longer sealed. The outside of the shell dripped in thin legs of blood. Her eyes followed out, and she saw the cape of Bogong. As she lifted it, she recognized the hand that had fed her figs on the most enchanted evening of her life.

The others arrived in the glade, and Luna rushed to her mother's side. Polyphemus and Atlas lifted their brother Bogong and laid him beside Morpho. The Queen and Luna wept for so much lost, and the men standing guard around them wept facing the valley of Lungomare

CHAPTER 54
"The Villa of Awareness"

Garbo entered the loggia of the Villa of Awareness and paused before the vista of Lungomare and the seated Theridiidae and Luna. "I am sorry for your loss."

Theridiidae traced the creases in her hands. Smoke rose from the villages along the beach and valley as she spoke. "The Oracles, the Heron, and the Fish, they looked at my hands, and they said prepare for losses. Losses, I heard that, and the story I told myself was much different from reality. I thought the loss of the grape harvest or a plague of locust and famine." She paused. "No, that's still a lie I'm telling myself." She looked up to Garbo. "The truth is that I thought we would lose some of the outer tribes, the coastal places. That those people, my people, would be enslaved. Taken from their homes, chained, raped, burnt, maybe even slaughtered. It was a trade I made in my mind. A trade that kept the Kingdom alive. A trade that I began to justify in my mind." The Queen stood and turned to the Giant Snail as if repentant. "I never thought losses would mean me. That famine would come to my table, and the organ meat of life would turn to ash. I didn't know that loss went so far as no hope. There is no hope of bringing him back to life. No bargain to be made, and if there were, who would I take it to? And yet now, I'm so vain as to feel my loss as greater than anyone else's." She raised her hands to the landscape around her and then looked back to Garbo. "I am sorry for your loss. Your Father saved our lives with his sacrifice. His shell will never be seen and heard with the other Ancient Kings along Lungomare."

"But his legend will ring in every ear for all eternity. Theridiidae, do you hear the voice of Morpho?" She stood and embraced Garbo with both hands and looked into his eyes.

"Constantly. And I hear his wings thrashing about in anger at being taken. He is angry. He's violent at this, this theft of our time."

"Has his country been notified, his people?"

"You mean Peru?"

Theridiidae closed her eyes and shook her head. Then, she covered her face with her hand to hide her embarrassment. "I never took it for real, you know? Now I'm seeing how much I discounted my husband. He was a King, greater and more powerful than I and yet, I tried to rule him. He ruled his country with all its gold and riches, possibly even greater than ours, and he did it all from away. He did it all while spending his life freeing slaves and giving them an opportunity to live in this beautiful place. Garbo, why did I do that? I wasted so much of our precious time trying to justify the story in my mind. How he was supposed to fit into my story. How he was supposed to be only for me. Now, look at the cost. A single man more remarkable than all the hosts I've known, and I could have ruled with him. Instead, I settled on trying to rule him."

"Theridiidae, maybe it's not too late. If you hear him, then he hears you. One power of grief is that it makes us honest with ourselves. When we are honest with ourselves, we can be honest with others and face reality. This is the Villa of Awareness, you asked to be here."

"The story I've been telling myself all these years is not true, and that realization is terrifying." She turned from Garbo and came to the side of Luna. The child reached out and took her mother's hand.

"Mother, Francis is seeking me."

CHAPTER 55
"The Lion's Den"

"Sevensthhh." A familiar hiss tickled the ear of the Orphan, and though he was in the dream state, he sensed something move in the shadows about him.

"Francis is my name." He lifted himself from a cot, and a drip of water fell to his forehead. He tasted it. "This water is spring water; it has never been in a wooden cask."

The hiss tickled the back of his neck. "This is not a ship." It moved past, and Francis waited for his eyes to adjust to the darkness before following its movements.

"I saw your ship, the black vessel, on the horizon. I saw the Eye of Knowledge beaming from its mast, and the Salt Lord was taking me, but this is Earth. Where are we? What is this place?"

"This is the Lion's Den, but don't worry, the old fellow died of thirst." Francis' eyes adjusted and saw chains and shackles on a prominent limestone surrounded by water in the underground cave. A match flickered, a candle was lit, and illuminated a slender face with reflective eyes. "Now then." It blew out the match.

"A cave of sandstone, we never left Terra Firma. We are in the dunes?" Francis could see the water dripping from the ceiling and the dark places green with saturated stone. The being slipped along those places. "I can still see your eyes. Could the Lion see your eyes when you watched him die?"

"I'm not going to kill you, Seven. You're far too valuable. Well, you could be. You know, I knew your father? Yes, si, claro. I knew him quite well." A cane-reed drew a distinguishable figure in the sand, and a smooth-soled boot swept the artwork away.

"Impossible, I'm an Orphan."

"Funny, so am I." The breath was hot against his ear, but the being was not there when Francis turned to see the face. "Would you like for me to tell you a story about him? I could tell you something, anything really, maybe why he chose to leave you? Doubtless, you've been wondering.

Before There Were Flowers

You know Morpho didn't give him much choice. Apple?" A tailored glove offered him the polished fruit from the darkness.

"Is that the one you offered Eve? You are the Prince of Lies, aren't you?" Francis's face was suddenly slapped.

"Prince of Knowledge is my name, and you'd do well to listen to my voice. Adam and Eve? I've nearly forgotten them, no, it was not an apple. Some hard fruit, really? No, it was a fig. Beautiful and sweet. I made good suggestions. I told them to work harder and be more conscious of their bodies. They needed clothes; they needed a purpose beyond silly pleasures. They were going to raise their children in a garden, huh, a garden? Can you imagine? Like goats. They thought their children were cherubim. I simply showed them that they needed to work hard to create something deserving of themselves. I was sad for them, truly. What happened and all that. They could have been rulers of empires if they had wanted it. Yet they constantly bickered back and forth. I'd hear their voices complaining over thorns, and cold, and the lack of meat. The difference, Seven, is that they were not born Gods like you and me."

"Was I born perfect?"

"No, no, not perfect, but I can make you thus. Your other people, the ones that have kept you slave by telling 'you're free'. They want to control you. I have knowledge Seven, and I've always been with you since you were a child. Doesn't my voice sound familiar? You've heard me in your mind. Praising you when you should be. Chastising you when your best attempts fail, stupidly. Morpho wanted your parents to be his slaves, and he wanted you to be his slave. He doesn't want you to think for yourself. Serve him, serve him, serve him and the Kingdom, for what? Do they share riches with you? Do you even know what the Greater Power is?"

Francis looked down and he realized he was on the prominent of limestone, with water passing by out of reach.

CHAPTER 56
"The Voice Of Knowledge"

"Seven, if you kneel and swear your allegiance, all this will be over. You will be like a God. That's what they don't want you to know. Your father knew this, and he loved you. Orphan was not your destiny. No, but they saw to that. Didn't they? Why else would they have taken you? Look here; it's been days since you tasted cool water. Let all this between us pass. You don't need to be chained up like something untamed. Kneel before me and fill this cup." Francis murmured in delirium. Took the servant's cup and held it up in the light of the moon.

"You keep talking to her, but it's been weeks. They've forgotten you. No worries, you didn't really need them." The Second Orphan pressed his hand against the heart-shaped quartz around Francis' neck. "How many True Artists would you like in your new Kingdom? When you bow to me, you will rule with me. This Kingdom? Do you want this part of Earth or another? Two? Hear my voice, Seven. If you can break stones with your hands, imagine what you can do with your words. People will bow to you, armies will serve you. Entire kingdoms will fear you. You, you, can be the new Belshazzar, no longer a forgotten disposable orphan, but a God, just like me. Riches, women, songs of glory written in your honor. Imagine the power we could wield over empires, Seven."

Francis turned the cup free, and it broke against the stones. Raising his head towards the cave ceiling, he received one drop of water as a reward.

"Seven! There's no meat in this for a Lion! Do you hear me? There's no place for you in this woman's desert! No one will serve you! No one! Look, this girl you keep calling out to she doesn't see your potential. Listen to the words of knowledge in your head and what my voice tells you. Don't be so stupid. You can't survive without me."

CHAPTER 57
"THE SIRENS OF SEA GLASS"

An attendant enters the loggia to wash the feet of the Queen. The sea glass palms of the young lady heat the water in the basin, and suddenly, the cool water steams. The Queen's eyes lift to meet the eyes of the siren. "Child, everything about you is enchanting but, look at me, you are in mourning."

"I'm sorry, my Queen."

The Queen looks deeper into the opal eyes and shakes her head. "No, no, Darling. You must not apologize for your grieving heart. If you do, then so must I."

"My lady, shall I wash these garments, stained with, with... the color red?" The Queen watched the foreign hand touch the silk scarf of Morpho. Another being innocent and yet taking him from her. Then she noticed the white silk against the pale skin of her hand and the palm of sea glass, warm, healing, and beckoning.

"I should serve you, child. I am your Queen and should be, therefore, a mother to you."

"No, my lady. It is my purpose here."

"How long have you and your people been in Gastropoda? You are the daughters of Eve, aren't you, the Sirens of Sea Glass? How did you come to live here?"

"Your husband, Mother. He delivered us from the Brine Earth. He, himself, read to us the Terms and Conditions of Freedom. I remember that day. Standing on the deck of The God of Peru and your King standing regal in the sunlight, his eyes such a color that we, the Sirens of Sea glass, born with adorned palms, were mesmerized by his love. Love not of us, or the sea, or the vessel but of you, my Queen. Do you know what it's like to long for a man who cannot be wooed? Young Hylas, when his vessel passed the Brine Earth, we swam out to him, singing, and pulled him from his bow perch. Swam that beautiful boy down and down among the sea-brown kelp, and not once did he cry out. But your Morpho was so faithful in heart and mind that we became captives." She returned her hand to the water, and it again heated around the feet of the Queen.

"Thank you. Thank you for telling me this. I see your hands, heating and cooling the waters, as they do. Is that how the Sirens of Sea Glass defend yourselves?" She reached down the arm to the elbow and lifted the young lady's hand from the water.

"No, we are women. We use our collective voices. The energy of our minds becomes intent in our palms, and we use the light from within us to temper the water so that our voice can be heard." The Queen touched the sea glass palm with her finger.

"The light within you united with intent becomes the Greater Power. Are you the daughter of Eve?"

"Eve is the mother of my mother. She was born outside the Mock Orange Hedge of Eden."

"Born outside of Eden? Is this why you are grieving child. Have you known loss again? Have you been, like I, suddenly cast out of Eden?"

"My Husband lives, Queen, yet he, he has lost those he loved, and what is more, he feels responsible. His heart is in such grief that neither my voice nor the touch of my hand can console him."

"He feels responsible? I am the one responsible. I brought this here to Gastropoda. I am the one to be punished, child." At this, the Siren of Sea Glass began to cry, and from those pools fell tear-shaped beads of warm glass into the Queen's hands. "Child, child, why does your husband feel guilty? Why is he punishing himself thus?"

"He sees with eyes like no other beyond the horizon of the new day and to the past of all our memories." And here, the Queen finished her words.

"But he only sees the truth. You are the wife of Atlas? You are the love he could not see coming? Quick, child, bring your husband to me."

Before There Were Flowers

CHAPTER 58
"MY DUTY"

Atlas, in orange and auburn, enters and kneels before the Queen, offering his sword to her. "My weapon Queen."

"And with this sword, I am to do what?"

"If you allow me, I will take my own life. It is the custom of my people in failure of duty."

The Queen took the sword of Atlas and slid the scabbard down the blade. The blue calligraphy of the sword's hilt reflected a life of service.

"Very well, remove your outer garment."

Atlas's eyes never lifted to meet hers.

The Queen stood, and with the blade, she pushed back the garment from Atlas's chest. "He marked you. This means he had faith in you." She studied the marking tattooed across his chest.

"But, I failed him, Queen. I did not deserve his trust, his admiration. I... I..."

"Did not deserve his love?"

The shock of this raised Atlas's eyes, and just as quickly, he lowered them, but not before the Queen saw the depth of his pain.

"I take responsibility. I should have seen this coming. I feel responsible."

"Why?"

"My vision has been clouded by love."

"And you intend to push love away and call it your duty to do so."

"It is my duty to serve the Kingdom and others, to provide, even if she cannot see that."

"Atlas, do you know how the Sirens of Sea-glass defend their kingdom from invasion?" His head twisted with mystery.

"They sing to them, offer comfort and rest, and then they put them under a spell."

"No, that is who they are, the blessed daughters of Eve. They use their voice. Tell me, Atlas, how well could you serve without this sword? How good would you feel about your service without this mark of trust? That woman who lies down with you and comforts your heart is the greatest weapon your life will ever know. You say that love has clouded your vision? I'd say all the cloudiness is all the light you have not allowed yourself to see through her eyes. Stand upon your feet." Atlas stood and looked into the eyes of the Queen. "This is the Villa of Awareness. Faith plus awareness is what surviving grief gives us. The awareness that love is not a distraction of duty but a glass with which all light not yet seen between the stars becomes visible."

 The Queen took the hilt of the sword and turned it upright between them. From her palm, she poured the tears of sea glass onto it. There formed a molten dome that she stuck against the mark of Morpho on his chest. "The faith you invest in doubt about yourself should never outweigh the trust others have placed in you."

CHAPTER 59
"A KINGDOM IS A BIRTHRIGHT"

"Seven, Seven, follow the drops of water." Francis squints his eyes against the sunlight. "Thirty-nine days in the Lion's den. You are no stronger, no wiser, not any richer. Look, it is me alone that helps you walk and stand. Here, come to me and see this." The clouds rolled upon themselves, shaping and cascading, then parting beneath their feet. Francis's eyes opened wide as he saw not only the Golden Kingdom but across the northern dunes past the Oracles of Heron and Fish to other Kingdoms of cities made of cut stone. "From this lofty height, you can observe your potential kingdom. Now this way." Francis's eyes turned, and again, the billows of the sky rolled away and looked down the slopes of the highest mountain over the piedmont to the sea. His sight flew like a condor over the seas to new lands with strange faces and names. "All this and more will be your empire. All faces will say your name and swear allegiance. Your birthright is a pathetic kingdom compared to this empire. With your powers, we can make the whole world surrender. Surrender to us or perish beneath the seas. Don't you like the sound of that? It makes no matter. The sea beasts will serve us too." He turned to face Francis again. "Gold can be harvested beneath the waves. We will control not only the land but also the great deeps. Just bow down and worship me. Apple?" Francis squared his shoulders and looked into the eyes of the snake.

"A kingdom is a birthright. An Empire is something you fight like hell for and eventually lose." The lofty peak beneath his feet crumbled, and darkness fell over the blue sky. The drip of water and the smell of old chains was reality. As his eyes adjusted to the darkness, he saw three stone sarcophagi with a symbol he knew well standing against the cave walls.

CHAPTER 60
"A Perfect Lie"

"What do you see, Atlas?"

"My Queen, the vision is unchanged. Many deep-keeled, dark ships, one larger than the others, all bear the banner of the eye."

"Can you discern their course?" Atlas turned toward her.

"The Golden Kingdom."

"Have you seen the sarcophagi of the other Orphans on board?"

"No, my Queen, they've disappeared?" She turned to the council assembled with her.

"Adonis, would you please tell me what the symbols of the burial chambers mean?"

Adonis stepped forward. "What do you know about Angels?"

"They are messengers of light."

"Yes, what do you know about fallen Angels?"

"They are messengers who cancel out light with lies. They are messengers of darkness."

"The Prince of Lies is collecting the relics of blind faith. The symbols are a series of keys and arrows. They represent knowledge and accuracy."

"He's constructing a perfect lie?"

"Every human has a message to tell. When we hear a message of darkness and believe it, that darkness becomes part of us. Our stories are no longer authentic, and we believe his lies."

"A lie that we are not good enough and do not deserve love that we must work, suffer, and put off happiness so that one day, we may deserve it. A lie that makes us judge ourselves and others as unworthy of forgiveness and incapable of love." She turned back to the vista and held her head in her hands.

"If we can see where he's taken relics of blind faith, it will lead us to Francis. Atlas, bring the Sirens of Sea Glass and reflect all the light in your eyes through their palms. When you find them, send Ulysses to The

Prince of Lies with a message of parlance."

"You intend to meet with him? He will have an advantage."

"I will meet him on neutral ground, in a place he is familiar with and feels empowered. Knowledge used in this way will be a useful weapon. I will meet him on the quarter moon in the garden of Gethsemane."

CHAPTER 61
"Free Will"

On the night of the quarter moon, the Queen slipped to the ground from a silver thread in the garden.

A groomed Prince in black velvet trimmed in greens and gold slithers between the foliage. "You always knew how to make an entrance, Theridiidae."

"Torchwood gives off a unique scent, she said."

The prince lifted a polished cane and sniffed. "Ahh, this stick? Funny story about this old sprig. This is the rod Aaron used to smite the rock in the desert. I gave it to him back then; well, I put it in his way, so to speak. I'd say he used it well, then, of course, tossed it aside rather quickly. A little memento, a relic, really; people don't realize how many are lying around. Now now, let me see, well, I'd say the legends are true. Look at you in this light! No wonder men are dying to sleep with you." He moved with grace and elegance. The subtle gold rings enhanced the buffed, clean fingernails protruding from soft cuffs. He rested against the limestone balustrade overlooking the sea. "You have only one ship these days? Lost some of your invisibility recently?" He turned and looked at her. "Wow, the pain is, it is, so beautiful inside of you, Darling." There was silence amongst the smell of earth and olive.

"Ironic, we meet here, in this place. I've been here before, and I suppose you knew that. This is where the Third Orphan was abandoned by his father. Ha, ha, you really must excuse my laughter; it's naughty when I think back. But I will be honest with you, I never really liked him. His Father used to go on and on in his court about how he was his only Son and had no heavenly mother. That he was born to do great things. To deliver the world, he had created. He would sit, staring at sometimes in the palms of his hands or other times as a mere footstool. Calling to his Son and saying, *'I have an idea, a way for us to play together in this game of Earth I created; what do you think about being the Savior of the World?'* And we all stood by as he showed him. *'This is how you walk on the water. And this is how to heal the sick and raise the dead ones. Fun, isn't it? Do you like it? Look here at this bit with loaves and fishes, and if you do it correctly, then later, the poor people will believe in you. See and they will lay down palm branches in the street for you to cross over the stones.'* The spoiled child would bring his wooden toys to the servant's table and ask to sup. Trying on their peasant sandals and stumbling on the kitchen stones. His Father would fetch him and call out, commanding the harpist to be quiet and the jesters to clear. He would bring him over and say, *'have you studied the game today? You know all Gods are excellent sportsmen. I've been thinking of a way for us to play it together. Now, you could enter the world as a King or a warrior and deliver them from some oppressor. That's just in my mind. What do you think you'd like to be there?'* And the son touched the blue and white globe with his toy and said, *'Father, may I make things of wood in a wood maker's shop? May I have a mother, and know her voice, and stirring at the dawning of each sun and hear her voice mingled with the Aeolian harps at night? Could I be a commoner there, sit at the servant's table, and know the sweet smell of the manger? Please, Father, it's truly what I want.'* You know it was clearly not what his father had planned, but then he had set it all in motion. The servants and us messengers had watched it all unfold. Seen the power of his creation grow and come to life and have a free will. That's when I knew it."

The Queen spun a silver thread in the branches between her hands. "What did you know, Lucifer? What knowledge did you glean?"

He turned and removed a neckerchief from his neck, revealing a handsome, smooth chest. "Is it hot here to you? Surprising how chills don't cool me like they used to." He paused and wiped his hands on the fine silk. "Free will. That's it. The old man didn't realize he even created that. He'd always say commands like, *'Let there be light and a sun to rule the day and a moon to rule the night.'* I approached him just then, extended my hand, and said, Apple? He took it without even looking at it, bit into it, and when the juices ran from his mouth into his beard, and I saw the throat swallow, I gasped. He turned and saw me. Saw me for the first time, not as a messenger to do errands but as someone he could believe in. It was possibly the greatest moment of my life."

"Not when you watched the son die?"

The prince took the cane and waved it in the air. "Ahh, that was an orchestrated moment, but no. I've always had the upper hand, you know, knowing what is inevitable. I really do try to tell people, and most do hear my voice, but then there are some." He pointed the stick towards her and then pirouetted. "No, my dear, I'd say a close second was right here, in this garden. Where was it now, exactly? Oh yes, just a slither away. That's when the father lost faith in his son, watched the game too long, and became too invested, and every step his son made did not match the story he had planned for him. Free Will became this anonymous player. The Father would thunder, and light would flash out of his eyes, so much so that he nearly drowned the son upon Galilee one time. With an apple in one hand, the old man stood above the World and raged at the actions of his Son, sleeping during the day, and then the Son stood up and used the lesson his Father had once so diligently taught him and walked upon the water and raised his hand and then uttered. 'Peace be still.' The Father threw the apple and turned his back on the world. He decided to change the parameters. If his Son was unwilling to be the Savior of the World, then he'd teach him a new lesson he'd never imagined before. That's when I knew I had won."

The prince stopped, took out calfskin gloves, tried them on, and removed them. He smiled broadly and looked at the beautiful Queen in the moonlight. "Pity the child had to die, but he was weak, and after all, it became the father's will. The truth is that I came and met with him here and presented him with a different strategy. He refused, of course. Wept and ultimately relinquished, *'not my will but thine.'* I could've used him, but the spoiled ones are always needy. No, I saw the greater picture. I had his tomb raided, his body stolen. I staged the appearance of him ascending into the heavens to his Father. Oh, the people, especially the poor and ignorant, oh, they ate it up. Relayed it as some big melodrama. Ha, ha, I mean, sometimes you win, and then you realize that it was just always meant to be. I tell people everything happens for a reason. They love that one too. Or that it was God's will. Oh, I do love that one, especially! Every time they believe it, I think of the old man losing control and throwing the apple. He lost interest, you know. He's probably moved on, created some new galaxy, and had another Son or Daughter. This world is all mine even he said so, that's why I'm in no hurry. I lie and wait; people usually do what I want without asking. You know we could rule it all together, but I'm sure that's not what you came to speak to me about, is it?"

The Queen stepped sideways and disappeared into the black night. The prince, intrigued, followed her with his handsome hooded eyes. "Did you come alone, Darling? That was our agreement. I really mustn't have to remind you. I expect everyone to be honest with me. Darling, what bargain did you seek with me?"

The silhouette of the Queen could be seen. "I came to offer my life for the liberation of Francis?"

"Francis? There are many in my service, but this name does not have any particular semblance. You wouldn't be speaking of the Seventh Orphan now, could you? Of course, not; that would be too much to ask. And your life, my dear, is, well, let us say, not as valuable as you think? I mean, yes, we could form a partnership, something of the H variety, a mutual agreement that is somewhat fragile. Ha, I mean, not everyone is impeccable with their word. But Darling, can't you see that it's destiny that soon I will kill you or stand by and watch others do it. And then how would it look for me to have partnered with a well-known whore? You're not even a True Artist; you're just sleeping with anyone and then, in your mind, considering yourself faithful. I don't understand your logic, but I admire your way of reasoning. Inspiring really. I've always admired the tenacity of a good slut. You know that's what your people say behind your back. Doubtless scared for their lives in the hands of a woman who must run off to the Oracles for consolation and direction. Do you wish upon stars, Darling? Cards or the lines in your hand? Imagine what your daughter thinks of you. I guess that's why she seeks heart advice from strangers. Those other women who are more stable than you? What do you think she thinks? Maybe you don't have it together like those other mothers? I'd say those mothers are there every night to hold them and tuck them in bed, but you, well, you are in bed with another stranger. What's wrong with the skin of your daughter? Why do you need that addiction of a faceless and nameless stranger? Fantasy? Is that the truth about your life, fantasy? She sees that better than any other." He left off, and the Queen looked inward.

"What would you do with Seven? Place him in your demon hole and torture his mind? Doubtless, you'd bed him. Even try to procreate your own powerful being. You wouldn't create that child for your own pleasure. To plat or to braid its hair? No, this one you'd play just like the old man. Groom it for your own game, and teach it to be your version of what is wrong and right. Now, the confusion is that you offered your life for him. I have to say I can't trust that because it is something I'd never do. You know by now the end of your Golden Kingdom is near. I've been slowly wrapping myself around it without your knowledge. Gradual pressure was slow at first, but now you're having trouble breathing. Soon, the drum beats of evading armies will be in your ears." He suddenly appeared in the face of the Queen. "You left your kingdom in the care of a whore! She sells herself to everyone! Did you really think Felionia would not sell herself to me?"

    The Queen stood behind the weaved veil amongst the olive branches. "Changing your mind now, Darling? Women have the right to capriciousness. It makes you a poor leader, but I can help you. I can save you. There's no other hope. Really, all is already lost. Listen to me, lend me, Luna, lend me your Kingdom, for a while, trust me, it will be no longer than a thought. I will bring Seven to the Eternal Fountain, and there Luna and Seven will produce a perfect child, and then another, and another. No one will see them there, but the legend will cover the Earth. A superior race, like Gods. Power, beauty, and intelligence living in the minds of the world. Not so bad, is it? Ruling the world just by making them feel inferior. The truth they will hear and believe is that they are not worthy. The entire world will be ruled from the house of Theridiidae. You will be the Spider Queen of the World; now, imagine sitting on top of that and wrapping your legs around it."

    The Queen slit the veil with the red blade and stepped forward. She kissed the lips of Lucifer passionately. "Oh, my dear. Yes, you do deserve to be Queen!"

CHAPTER 62
"Messengers of Light"

"Adonis, did you build this lens?" Atlas courses along an invention resting on a gun carriage. "It's shaped like a canon, and yet it is..."

"Capturing all the light we cannot, see? It's a telescope, but not just a telescope; it's ah, how would you say?"

"Made from King Bianchi's shell, isn't it?"

"Yes, yes, it is. The children, I never knew they adored him or even knew him, and yet after the attack, they ran to the place of the pinnacles and filled their garments with the remnants of his polished shell. I asked myself who must have told them to do this, but then I answered my question. Love. He used to walk with them along Lungomare, and he'd say, *'Suffer not the children to come unto me, for thus is their kingdom.'*"

They brought all the shattered pieces to me, and I knew not what to do with them. I closed my eyes and touched his shell once again. In the moment, I saw myself as a child holding the hand of a Janissary from the house of the great Sulieman. He had, yes, been trained to kill and murder at will, but that had not defined his life. He had given himself to the artistry of buildings and devoted his mind to math and memory. He saved not only my life but that of The Great Standing Army. Building bridges where others had failed. Then palaces, and eventually mosques. He took me in, not out of pity or charity but rather as an apprentice. He gave me a room and food and parchment with ink and one day said, *'write this down. All art is created in a series of measured movements. Complete each measured movement in its entirety before going on to the next. The inescapable result of your work will be art.'* He did not tell me what I was in the world. He did not say you are just a child or label me as a boy destined to be a servant or some Queen's eunuch. No, what he did was show me that I was an artist free to live and create in any way I chose. He gave me the Terms and Conditions of Freedom without me even realizing it. I used the lessons he taught me in math and magnification. Using the polished shell of Bianchi and the sea glass lens, it captures all the future light that has yet to be seen and can reflect that hope around the world. Its greatest potential is when the eyes of the child look through it. Come, tell me what you can see, Atlas." Atlas moved to the end of the telescope and looked with contemplation into the eyes of Adonis.

"I can see beyond the horizon of the new day, and there are many sails."

"Are they dark sails from the deep-keeled ships?"

"There are so many masts. It's like a great forest marching on the dawn of a new day. And their bows hold golden spheres reflecting the sun's light. It's the Peruvian Navy!" He lifted from the telescope to look with his own eyes. Then he turned to Adonis. "I cannot see them with my eyes, and I can only see the black ships at hand. Is this true? Is this something we can believe in? Atlas looked into the Bianchi lens again. "I want to go with you, Adonis, into battle. I'm ready at a moment's notice. I'm prepared even to never return."

"No one doubts that Atlas, but let me ask you, does the grape ever say to the root of the vine, be more like me?"

"I don't understand the metaphor. I'm a warrior, I should be with you in the battle."

"This is not one battle. This is an ongoing war for the entire world. Rather than thinking yourself a single warrior, I'd rather you think yourself a General leading intelligence."

"What do you mean?"

"Look into the Bianchi glass again, but this time cast your gaze to the Earth's four corners." Atlas looked again. "Record here what you see and when you see it."

"Wait, what's this? There are beings, some human, and some animals, that use different ways to reflect light; they are messengers of light and angels. The Peruvians use their art forms, the gold spheres, the Sirens of Sea Glass in the Brine Earth, which hold their palms towards the sun, and light spectrums flood the sky. The glaciers at both poles are brilliant, and now, oh my." He lifted his eye from the lens and looked towards the heavens. "The mighty condors, the great protectors of the Spirit Fire, are above us, and their eyes reflect through sculptural shells here along Lungomare."

Adonis stepped over and placed a hand on the glass. "This lens was built for you. Look again, please, but this time with a Condor's eyes, and tell me again what you see."

Atlas peered once more. "It can't be. How is this possible? I need more hands to write this down. Adonis, is this?" Adonis placed a hand on his shoulder.

Before There Were Flowers

"Do not doubt yourself again. Your heart led you here for this purpose. Your eyes see only truth, and you're right; you need ledgers of truth to write down your vision."

"When I asked to see with the eyes of a Condor, my eyes began to fly over and around the entire Earth. If I asked to go higher, I could nearly touch the stars, but more shocking is that I could see myself on the highest peak of Gastropoda, looking into the future."

Adonis stood back and smiled. "Very good, very good. Come sit with me. When we think our loved ones have given us all the gifts of their lives, they surprise us most after their passing. Bogong once mentioned that he wished to be remembered for peace, not war. I desire to honor him and give his name to this place, but I hear his faithful voice in the wind saying, *'peace hill.'*"

"We will need to protect the Bianchi lens. The Priest and the Prince of Knowledge will all seek this instrument."

"Yes, you're right. Ha, exactly. Employ masons to build stone towers here and everywhere across the Island. Give them the appearance of sugar mills, plant crops, and harvest them. Build fires when the season arrives. Most of all, hide the glass and commission the Keeper of Bees to fill the voids in the stone with hives. Now, then, let's talk about this battle."

CHAPTER 63
"Faith Plus Awareness"

"Seven, Seven?" The prince snapped his fingers in the face of Francis. "Did you miss me? Still not eating apples, are we? We have company. Are you excited? Come now, are you hearing me?" He poured water into a wooden bowl. "You know, taking a little water to preserve your life is not wrong. You'll die in here unless you listen to me. Well, to us. Our friend is here, and she'll tell you the news. Oh, too soon for you, Darling? Should I tell him?" Francis opened a beleaguered eye. "She cuts a wonderful figure even in this dim light, don't you agree?" Francis saw the shape of the Queen, her shoulders and thighs, and places where her red swords should have been. The Queen turned her eyes away.

"You see Seven. It's over. The big lie is done now; it's not your fault. Well, some of it. When was the last time you saw Morpho and Bogong? Ahh, yes. I remember. You know I wasn't in the deep-keeled ship with the Eye. This Eye." He lifted a chain, and an amber eye fell against the silk shirt. "No, no, I was on the cliff above you. I needed proof, you see. I wanted to see it with my own eyes. You know how you would react, and all, when the catalyst was near. I assumed you would destroy the Earth. I assumed you would've destroyed everyone there. Well, you did kill your friends. Oh, don't you remember?" He leaned forward and touched the stubbled chin of the young man. "Apple?" He washed it in the cool water of the bowl. "No, no, is it too painful? Knowing that you have this gift, that people liked you, and you mistakenly killed them? Not some glancing blow but, but, well, Bogong will never be returning to his wives and children. That The God of Peru no longer has a worthy Captain. That your efforts were fruitless, even Gastropoda was a figment of your imagination. Look at me." He snapped loudly. "I've tried so hard to tell you the truth."

Loud explosions could be heard, and the rock of the Lion's den shook off dust from its form. "Ha, further proof! The battle for the Golden Kingdom has begun. Those are missiles from many deep-keeled ships, my ships." The ground shook again. "More people are dying because of you. Is that what you want? Kneel before me, and this can all be over."

Francis lifted his chains and dropped his head. A single ray of light illuminated his blonde hair and shoulders. "Listen to me, Seven, this is how the world is; embrace it, relish in it." He stood and spun to look for the Queen. "Darling? Where are you? Come into the light, will you? I'm going to need your seduction techniques here. Now, Seven. There's another matter, one I don't think you've considered in light of all this. You see, it's a bit sticky." He licked the apple juice from his fingers. "She will never love you, not now, I mean, I know that you didn't mean to kill him. You still don't remember? How you took his life in front of her eyes? You nearly killed her. My heart was racing. I saved her, well, her mother, and I." He reached behind him for her hand, but it was not there.

"I asked you to come here!" His voice commanded in the halls of the cave. "Don't you see now, Seven? The greater power that they were keeping from you? Have you figured it out?" The missiles shook the Earth.

"Ahh, Peruvian guns. Your foolish friends, undoubtedly desperate now, have arrived. Only to be defeated and worse, of course, unless you stop it."

Francis stirred at the sound of the different guns. He shook the dust that fell from his braids. His voice had become deeper with the lack of water. His arms twitched at the dust, and veins could be seen as he lifted the heavy chains with ease. He shook his head.

"Sorry, I just caught the last part about the Greater Power. Have you been talking long? You see, Devil, I've been dreaming. I heard nothing you said, just the whirl of those glorious guns." The chair slid back as the prince took in the physical change happening. "You asked if I knew what the greater power was? Is that correct?" He shook the sleep from his head again, and the light illuminated his eyes, and his stubble had turned to thick beard. "The Greater Power is faith plus awareness." His voice filled the air. The prince slid backward and began to stand.

"No, no, no, no! That is not it! Slut, where are you? Come here, come here! He ran to the Queen in the shadows and pulled her by the hair to the face of Francis, still bound in chains. "You tell him, you magnificent Whore that it's over that I have won! That this Earth was given to me to rule! Tell him, you worthless bitch! Tell him what the Greater Power is." He shook the Queen, and her face turned ashen; her mouth opened and closed, and she stammered.

"Well, you see, Sir, I'm just a simple Queen, a leader of simple people, not a diviner." The prince's eyes dropped, and his head turned towards the words.

"Moglie!" like the sword of Zeus, his hand flew, and the suit of armor was rent, revealing the mark of Morpho! "He fucking trusted you!" He kicked Moglie's body across the room into the sandstone columns.

"No, no, no, no, this will not do! You belong to me! I will never leave!"

Francis' arms were bulging, and hair covered his forearms.

"No, you do not! This is not happening!"

Francis' shirt ripped, and his thighs began to split the sewn fabrics of sailor pants. He lifted and smashed the chair beneath him.

"The Greater Power is within me! My faith plus awareness is all I need." Francis stood in the light, illuminating him. His hair was growing down his back, and his eyebrows were deepening. His jaw was protruding, and teeth of ivory could be seen."

"What else? You know you're not enough. You're not perfect, and you will never will be, orphan."

Hair grew over Francis' clutched fist, and claws emerged from his mighty arms. "Intent!" The chains burst and flew away, and the prince shielded himself from the light radiating from the Lion's breast.

"You died here once, orphan, you will die again if you do not believe me!"

Francis opened his mouth, and the spear of light became his dream state with the world. "Suffer not the little children to come unto me."

Atlas turned to all the orphans in Gastropoda. "Now, children! Gather all the light we have not yet seen."

From beyond the horizons of the new day, the golden spheres, the shells of snails, the palms of sea glass, the glaciers of the far north. The light beat along with every butterfly's wing, and like a pebble thrown into a still pond, a wave rolled toward the armadas and armies of darkness.

"No, no, no, no, this was not my plan!" The prince was hurled like the ships and sea monsters of all evil.

Francis caught the sound of the light and reflected it again, and the stone walls of the Lion's den blew apart. The prince shielded his eyes from the light, and staggering, he drew his sword from the old cane and fell against the debris. "You worthless pig!" He spit on Moglie in his original sailor form. "I will never leave you, Francis. Whatever you call yourself means nothing. I will return and destroy you." He leaped from the cliffs, slapped the water, and began to swim half under half on top of the remaining ship.

CHAPTER 64
"Commander of Tides"

The God of Peru plunged into the blue waters of the Caribbean Sea. "Come in."

Adonis opened the door to the Captain's Quarters and stepped inside. Francis set at Morpho's charting desk. "You're really going to keep this look? The hair, the shirt unbuttoned and all the muscles."

Francis looked up. "Ha, ha, that is the first funny I've ever heard you try to make."

Adonis, in royal blue, smiled back peacefully.

"Are we on course for the Priest and the Orphanage?"

Adonis nodded.

"It's on the horizon. Have you found anything useful in the desk? I'm here for you if you have questions."

Francis drew a purse of gold coins from the drawer. He poured them on the table in the shape of his hand, and each coin clung to a fingertip. "The golden spell Morpho cast on me that day in the market." He looked up to Adonis and received validation of a memory. So, all of these likenesses on the coins have been captains of ships like this? Doing this business? Such powerful titles, names and figures are written here."

"You know they are calling you The Commander of Tides." Francis looked up to his teacher. "However, I assume that your coin will need space not only for your face but that of Luna?"

Francis smiled as he swirled his hand and dropped each coin back into the purse. "Yes, and, well. We are going to need a space on deck for children."

Adonis's face lit up. "Really! Congratulations!"

The bells rang, and they stood to walk on the forward deck.

"Polyphemus, has everyone been removed from Orphanage?

"Yes, Captain, they're safe aboard."

"Everyone?"

"Well, Sir. There is a rather priestly rat still in there."

"Very good. Fire at will."

The God of Peru, under full sail, rolled on her side and released a broadside of canon fire across the sea, destroying the Orphanage of the Priest.

"Francis, do you know the name of your Father? He was a Caribbean planter, no?" Francis had taken Luna in his arms, his hand on her belly. He looked up.

"His surname was Drake; why do you ask?"

"The coins. I assume one day some Kingdom will make a Pirate like you royalty. What would they call a complicated explorer like you? Sir Francis Drake has a ring to it."

Before There Were Flowers

CHAPTER 65
"The Dream State"

"Bonjour, Maria. Mon petite Champi."

"Bonjour, Maman."

Come now, turn toward me. A kiss. How's the fever?" The child left her finger pressed to the glass where a snail hung. "Is Garbo still sleeping?" The blue eyes of the child connect to the mother's. "Oh no, Maman. Do you remember? A Snail Day is much longer than ours he just moves slowly."

"And yet every night you search for him, in what's his home called?"

"Gastropoda, Maman."

"Oh, yes."

"He's been telling me a wonderful story. If I touch his shell here, like this, we dream together."

The Mother forced worry of fever, into a smile. Her eyes wander the sick bed. "Your sketches. You painted everything with this one fine brush? So many characters. Butterflies and Moths. These names? Where did you learn their names? Atlas, Ulysses. Why is this bit of parchment empty, just a name, Bogong? That's a wood moth but why no painting, ici?" The child placed her hand on her mothers.

"He's there, Mother. You just have to talk to him and ask him to appear. You see, He's hidden, like courage." She looked to her child's face for assurance.

"The Blue reminds me of the sea here in Ortigia. I shall open the windows for you to see along Lungomare." The Mother lifted her skirts and unlocked the wide fenetres, revealing the outer walls of the city and the azure waters of the Ionian Sea.

"How does Papa say it?" The child spoke. "Lungoish Marish?" The Mother stopped and smiled. "Does he have pearls in his mouth, Maman?"

"No child, but he is Spanish, in love with another land and language.

When I first saw him, though, he did have small pearls braided into his beard. I will never forget him riding his thundering horse off the gangplank of his ship into the market streets of Venice. Pegasus was his name. He rode ducking under archways and crossing bridges, an Aeolian harp slung across his back like a wing."

"I love that story, Maman. Will you sit here and tell it to me again?"

"Fish, for sale."

"It's him! The Orphan. Lower the basket for him! Oh, the coins, Maman! Don't forget." The child sat up in bed, and the colorati of the sea danced across her eyes. "Kittens, Maman! Look at them gazing down from the balcony into the garden. They always appear when I need them, like guardians."

"Would you like to spend the day there, in le jardin? Polyphemus would be so happy to see his playmate again. Maybe after the doctor comes, no?" The child turned back toward the snail and placed her finger against the glass. "Mon Champi? Pourquoi n'amimez-vous pas le medecin? Why do you not like him?"

"He whispers, Maman, and wears those dark clothes and that cane. The potions he pulls from the dark-keeled bag. He always closes the windows, tells me stay in bed. He says I'm not strong enough. He doesn't know me." She turned away and traced the edges of Gastropoda. "Garbo says that we are made of light."

"I think of Papa, sailing upon The God of Peru. What it must feel like for him to see us here in the Villa of Consapevolezza, and yet he's at anchor offshore waiting for us to give a signal. Is today the day?"

"Oui, Mon petite Champi!" The Mother lifted and took a white sheet, and the infant kittens clung to it and then released. She waved it like a flag from the balcony in flowing streams." Cannons saluted.

"Peruvian guns, Maman! Papa is coming home. Tell me again, Maman, have you always loved him? Tell me again how he fought for you?" The Mother takes a cool cloth from the basin and places it on the child's forehead.

The child closes her eyes. "You sleep and dream so deeply, child. Look who's here! Polyphemus, and of course, your wooden sword!" She opens her sleepy eyes, and the dog scatters the kittens. She snuggled the dog, "My protector."

"Are you ready to leave this shell of a room, Darling? Your teacher

Adonis has a new telescope in la piazza vicino alla Duomo. He says it collects all the light we cannot yet see of the future and the time Before There Were Flowers."

THE END

EPILOGUE

The Island of Sicily is the most invaded piece of land in the world. Its people are diverse, like each city. This is my home; being so close to the sea nurtures my soul.

This story was written in my apartment in Ortigia, Siracusa, in Sicily. I would wake up each morning, sit at the kitchen table, and write everything I had dreamed of. When I hit a spot in the writing where I needed clarification of the correct direction, I would stop and walk around the city. My apartment on the island is one hundred feet from the sea in either direction. Arethusa Spring is just feet away. I often take my paddle board and tour the sandstone caves and springs in the city walls and around the Castello Maniace. Being in this beautiful and historic city brought so much character to this book.

Every character in the book is an actual historical figure taken from history. I gave every figure an animal characteristic. All the character's names are the names of their metaphorical self. Gastropoda is the name for a Snails habitat. Theridiidae, is the name of a spider. Morpho, Adonis, Atlas, Bogong, all names of moths or butterflies. Moglie, is the word for wife in Italian.

Queen Nsinga of Ndongo was a natural person. Morpho's character is based on Lope de Aguirre.

My ideas for the Salt Lord and the Sirens of Sea Glass came from harvesting sea salt and sea glass from the Ionian Sea.

For the past two years, I have struggled with a lung disease. I have been in and out of cardiac arrest and spending a lot of time on the cancer ward of the hospital. Any type of lung disease can cause you to become very fatigued and emotional and to have incredibly vivid and intense

·

dreams. While writing this book, there was about a six-week period where I spent sixteen hours a day, dreaming. I dreamed the majority of this novel. I would then sit at my kitchen table and write down everything I had dreamed. Then, I would return to dreaming. This is not what I wanted to do or how I wanted to spend my life. I simply had no choice. However, I used the power of those dreams to create this work.

Many people have died before their time or were killed without having fulfilled their life work. These people often visit my dreams for months at a time and tell me their stories. I'd like to know whether I am supposed to just listen or if I am supposed to tell their life stories. While writing this book, an Italian immigrant visited my dreams for about six months. He has a very beautiful story. He told me about an Aeolian harp. Once I wrote those words into this book, it fulfilled his need, and he has not revisited me. I would like to acknowledge the life of Salvatore Campagna.

I would encourage anyone who feels they are slaves to events out of their control to use the greater power within them to create good from evil.

Credits

In this book, I used a lot of what Don Miguel Ruiz teaches us about life in his books. His book The Voice of Knowledge has made a difference in my life. Thank you for your life's work. I share that wisdom in hopes of helping others.

I used parts of love poems from Pablo Neruda during Polyphemus's remembering of Mary and Christ's crucifixion, where she talks about his feet.

The character of the Queen was based on Nxinga's life in Ndongo. Her character will be further developed in the sequel to this novel.

The character of Morpho was based on the life of Lope De Aguirre.

The character of Bogong was created after reading about relationships and marriage customs in Ethiopia.

The character of Adonis was created after visiting Istanbul and the Palace Museum. His character was taken from my own life experience. Twelve years after my wife died, I met Kerri, with whom I could walk together in Gastropoda on this Earth. The character of Adonis will be explored more in the sequel.

The character of Atlas. I did not know he was of Japanese descent until the moment he offered to take his own life for what he perceived as a failure in his duty.

The character of Ulysses was left undeveloped for the sequel to the novel.

The character of Luna was based on what I dream about of my own daughter if she had not died. Her character will be developed in the sequel of this book.

The characters of the Salt Lord, Swan Lord, and Sirens of Sea Glass will all be developed in the sequel to the novel.

The character of Pegasus came from my own love for the beauty of horses. I lived in Beaufort, NC, before it became known. It was a sleepy little fishing village with a small, protected Island, Carrot Island, in front of it and home to about eighty wild horses. During my sculptural career, I decided to do a series of stone sculptures honoring these horses. I spent countless hours in the marshes of Carrot Island in a canoe, sketching the various wild horses. That time of my life was beautiful. Shackleford Banks is home to nearly three hundred wild horses. Currently, I have a white and black horse named Amore that lives in my olive grove on Mt. Etna in Sicily. He loves to run and jump and follows me everywhere while I'm working.

The character of Francis came to me while living in St. John, USVI. Every day and every night, I observed the Sir Francis Drake channel, and that got me interested in his life.

At the very end of the book, I learned what animal character trait Francis would have, and it was revealed to me in the moment just as it was to the readers.

The Princess of Cats is written to honor sex workers around the world. The reference to them as True Artists and revered parts of a community is how I feel they should be honored. Sex is not the original sin. It is just as essential as salt and bread. I do not like that the world today, or at least in the United States, has made sex taboo and something dirty. It has created a cancer within loving relationships in the United States that will cost us dearly. Other countries have not believed the lie that sex or sexual pleasure is a sin. People who love one another should be at liberty to express love. The expression of love for a partner is a beautiful and healthy thing. It is a small and perfect gift, and it is all yours.

This book, at one time, was going to be called The History of Peru. I became fascinated with its incredible history. To tell it correctly, you must start in Venice, Italy. I started this novel but still need to finish it. Instead, I incorporated some points into this book. The country of Peru is understated at this time of the World. That will not always be the case. When the World was last destroyed, Peru was a place where the gods chose to start the world over. There is vast wisdom and great secrets held beneath its sand and soil.

This book was written in Ortigia, Siracusa, Sicily. I have so much to say about it that I don't know where to start. In May 2024, I moved back to Italy. I knew that I wanted to go to Sicily, but I was not sure where, so I rented a car and began to drive. I had read a bit about Ortigia, and I knew it was calling me, so I pushed it off.

When I got there it was an immediate feeling of being home. I stayed for a few days and then left. It was still calling me, so I returned for a more extended period.

I have worked my entire career as a sculptor of stone. Every sculpture of stone has a mark that the Sculptor puts in the stone that identifies the work. It is like a brand you see placed on cattle. Some are similar, but no two are the same. I have worked my entire career under a unique symbol.

I rented an apartment in Ortigia for one year. I began to walk its streets and look at its artwork. I started to recognize the traits of a sculptor who lived and worked in my neighborhood. I visited the local museum, and his work was displayed. It is unique in its form, over exaggerating certain sections of his work while still maintaining the mathematical equation that every eye sees as beauty.

Moreover, he covered the outside of his work with his symbol; most are hidden. He wanted someone to make no mistake of who it was that created this work. Later that week, I was walking by the waterfront marina, and here was another work of this artist covered in his symbol. Evidently, he lived in the building where I rented my apartment. His symbol is the same exact one I have worked under my entire career. His form is my form. His apartment is my apartment. Just as Adonis has lived for centuries. Ortigia has been my home before in another lifetime. I want to thank the beautiful people of this city who have welcomed me home with open arms.

Many people have died before their time or were killed without having fulfilled their life work. These people often visit my dreams for months and tell me their stories. I'd like to know whether I am supposed to just listen or if I am supposed to tell their life stories. While writing this book, an Italian immigrant visited my dreams for about six months. He has a very beautiful story. He told me about an Aeolian harp. Once I wrote those words into this book, it fulfilled his need, and he has not revisited me. I would like to acknowledge the life of Salvatore Campagna.

Salve, If you want me to tell the story of your life, you must visit me again. If I take your story and try to finish it, it will be a distorted version. If you tell it to me, it will be the truth. I will only write the truth.

On January 1, 2024 Kerri and I wrote our names on a piece of paper with a few vows. The wedding contract was good for one year with the option to renew. Sometimes, just like Adonis we hope for things. When they manifest it can feel too good to be true. Men and women both begin to protect their hearts. For me it goes a step farther. Everyone that I have ever loved has died. Facing my pain and fear and taking a step towards love was faith and awareness mixed with intent. Kerri has been the treasure of my life. You see, I thought that loves light for me was all burned out. I was okay with that but I was lonely. I asked the world for a chance to love again. I wanted an A type relationship. The universe gave me that in Kerri.

I want to thank Kerri Rachelle for editing this entire book. She did this without asking me. She knew this is where I struggle the most and she just did it. This act of love and kindness and appreciation for my life's work is beyond my words. This is an act of love, and it means the world to me.

Made in the USA
Columbia, SC
31 January 2025